BLACK GIRL LOST

Written By:

DEMETRIA POOLE

TABLE OF CONTENTS

Prelude

In the roughest projects in the Atlanta, Georgia area, lived three young girls. They became best friends from the very beginning. They were Shari Parks, Chocolate, Jalisa Brown, Lee-Lee, and Raven Smith, Redbone. Chocolate was the baddest young thang in the hood. She was like a mocha brown complexion with smooth skin that could put one in the mind of Nia Long. She was indeed everything all the other chicks in the hood wanted to be. With her banging body and beautiful face, Chocolate had all the big ballers in the hood chasing after her. Unlike all the other girls that just wanted to be noticed, Chocolate knew how to use what she had to her advantage. In order to fuck with her campaign, you had to ride in the flyest car and keep a stupid bankroll. Chocolate's best friend was just as beautiful as she was, and they too had every guy on the blockheads turning every time they walked by. Redbone was light brown skin, slim waist with a nice size ass, small breast, and average height. Redbone was the total opposite of Chocolate and Jalisa. She wasn't a savage. She was a kind-hearted, lovable person. Redbone's sweet loving personality was her blessing as well as her curse. Jalisa always fussed that Redbone's biggest downfall was that she always fell in love so easily and loved too hard. Jalisa and Chocolate were somewhat alike; they only wanted the money, the jewels, and the most expensive brand of clothing and shoes. The two of them weren't looking for love; they were so cutthroat. They were only in it for the money, glitz, and glamor. Jalisa was that one friend that was always loud and ghetto. Her hair and nails stayed laid to the gods with the brightest colors, no matter the season. Jalisa had no filter on her mouth, whatever came to her mind, came out her mouth without a second thought. Due to the fact she had a smart mouth, she stayed in some drama. She could hold her own, so she didn't mind fighting. Chocolate oftentimes would fuss at Jalisa about being so ghetto and boyish. Chocolate's famous slogan to Jalisa was, "Ladies are to be seen not heard, Jalisa." Chocolate always carried herself in a much older and mature manner. Her demeanor had almost everyone she met puzzled as to how old she truly was. Although she was built like a grown woman, she was only sixteen when people started to notice her developing body.

Chapter one

Chocolate

As a child growing up in the projects, it got hard to manage at times, and the living arrangements in which I lived weren't really ideal. I remember nights I had to hide under the bed from gunshots ringing outside my bedroom window. While I was under the bed, I would sometimes pray to God to get me out that hell hole. Despite how hard I prayed, God wasn't working fast enough, so I came up with a plan to get myself out. You see, I didn't always have this stunning body, fancy wardrobe, and ballers flocking to me. Once I discovered that I could use what I had to get what I wanted and deserved, I did just that. Back when I was younger in grade school, I was a lame nerd that nobody paid attention to. The boys always picked at me because I wore glasses, and my mom always plaited my hair in the same two pigtails daily. I never understood why she didn't do more to my hair, being that she knew how to do hair. She always complained that I had too much hair, and I was too tender-headed, so she didn't want to be bothered with it. Momma was the neighborhood stylist. She used to do hair out the kitchen as her side hustle just to make ends meet. So, you would think that she would have more tolerance for her own child. Due to my nerdish ways, the girls in school would try to fight me as well, but I wasn't afraid to fight them. I just chose not to fight in school. Education was too important to me. I was also terrified to get suspended from school because Momma didn't play when it came to academics. She always stressed it to my siblings and me that without education, we wouldn't make it far in life. She would always say, "Education first and everything else comes after that." Despite all the bullying I experienced, I was able to steer clear of the principal's office. That was right up until third grade. Michelle had pulled my hair for the last time. From kindergarten until now, she had been bullying me for some odd reason. I never bothered her or anyone in her crew, so I didn't know what her issue was. But I was fed up.

That day, I politely got out of my desk, turned to her desk directly behind mine, and dragged her out of her desk. She didn't see it coming. I walloped her, blood flew out of her mouth. The class was in an uproar. Everyone was yelling some sentiment for me to beat her and other things they were afraid to do themselves. I pushed her over the desk and got on top of her, throwing punch after punch. I wrapped my hands up in her too small to make a ponytail hair, attempting to get a good grip on her. I could feel Mrs. Tolbert trying to pull us apart. I continuously rammed her head into the floor. I was in such a rage everyone seemed to disappear, but I could hear Jalisa yelling, "She's bleeding, let her go! Let her go! That's enough, crazy!" I had had enough of her bullshit, and everyone else's shit too. So, at that moment, I took all my frustrations out on her. I had so much built-up tension. I was so angry and fed up with the bullying that all Momma's preaching about school and academics was right out of the window. Although you couldn't tell by looking at me, things at home weren't squeaky clean. I was sleep-deprived and exhausted because my mom had been up bitching all night, so I was in no mood to deal with Michelle's bullshit. Finally, Mrs. Tolbert, along with Ms. Nash from the English class across the hall, was able to break us apart. Ms. Nash had me pinned to the wall while Mrs.

Tolbert took Michelle to the nurse because she was bleeding all over the place. It took several minutes for me to calm down, and finally, I was able to answer the millions of questions I was being asked. I was taken to the principal's office, eventually. Once I was seated, he went on and on about how harsh my punishment could be, being that Michelle was bleeding and beaten up so badly. However, I only received a three-day suspension instead of being expelled because I reported to Mrs. Tolbert several times that Michelle and a few other girls were bullying me. It wasn't my fault she didn't report it to her boss or do what she was supposed to do as the teacher. Momma was pissed that I was suspended. The whole way home, she bitched about how she should beat my ass for being suspended. It wasn't like I was missing any classwork because all my teachers sent these ridiculously thick packets home for me to complete. I tried to explain to her that the girl and her friends were picking on me every day, and I was fed-up with it. During those three days, I sat home, wishing that I didn't have to be there. I wanted to be anywhere but in the projects. I felt like I didn't belong, and somehow God sent me to the wrong uterus. As bizarre as it sounds, I was so sure of that. The last night of my suspension, Momma came to my room and gave me this long speech on how I should block out what people say long as they didn't put their hands on me. I had tried that for as long as I could. I had to show them bitches I wasn't the one to play with. Don't let this cute face and my short stature fool you! I was a force to be reckoned with. From that day forward, I didn't have any problems out of the class bullies. Upon my return to school, they all wanted to be friends with me, actually. I wasn't really the friendly type, so I wasn't into making friends. The fight was the talk of the school for at least two/three weeks. I didn't have friends because although I was young, I figured out that a bunch of girls hanging together spelled trouble. I tried to stay out the way of troublemakers. The remainder of the year, I stayed to myself. I was such a loner. I walked the halls alone, and during recess and things like that, I would sit alone, reading and or writing poetry. It was a passion of mine to read. During the reading, I would pick my favorite character and pretend I was that person. It was my escape from my harsh reality. It was fun and exciting to be someone else and to go to different places in my mind. Some of the places I would visit through the books were angelic, and some were repulsive. With third grade approaching the end of the year, I was somewhat terrified of going to fourth grade. I'm not quite sure why it seemed so scary being that I had been transitioning through school with that same group of kids since kindergarten. Maybe it was the meeting and getting to know new teachers who probably wouldn't understand me and my weirdness. I knew that regardless of how frightened I was, I had to move on to the next level, and I had better prepare myself. Although I wasn't the friendly approachable type at times, I kind of wished I had friends to make the process of transitioning to a new grade level easier and a little less scary. Third grade came to an end, and it was summertime. I hated being out of school because it presented too much free time for children to get into trouble. I remember sitting on the back porch one cool night in June of that year, reading my book when a group of boys simultaneously met up at the playground. At first, everything seemed cool. They were just talking normal or at least that's what I thought because my head was buried too far into my book. That was until I heard the pitch of their voices getting louder and louder. I tried not to make any sudden moves because I was slightly scared. I just continued to watch the altercation unfold. When I saw Ant-man pull out a black and silver gun, I gasped for air, dropped my book, and covered my mouth to muffle my scream. As I was trying to ease my way into the house, gunfire erupted. I could hear the bullets hitting the metal poles on the playground set. I fell into the house, yelling and screaming in panic. I was uncertain how long the gunshots were going on for, but it seemed like they were never-ending. I lay on the floor of the living room, praying to God for it to stop. Shortly after my last, "Please, God, let it stop," the gunfire finally stopped. I lay on the floor for a while after it stopped just to be sure it was really over. Then finally, I ran upstairs to Momma's room and crawled underneath her covers, scared for dear life. The police and ambulance sirens could be heard in the distance, and the closer they got, the heavier my breathing became. I was so frantic, and all Momma kept saying was, "Where the hell is Daddy?" I just remember lying there, hoping that Ant-man or none of the other boys saw me because that could put me in a bad situation. I stayed in the house all day the next day because I was terrified to run into one of the boys just in case my presence didn't go unnoticed. Out the back window, I could see the playground was taped off with crime scene tape. I figured someone died because they had to shoot well over a hundred bullets the previous night. As I was pulling my head back in the window, I could hear someone asking who lived in my apartment, so I ran to my room to hide. Momma was yelling my name, but I refused to move from my hiding spot to see what or who was at the door. I could hear a lady's voice as well as a man's voice, but I still wasn't going to walk down the stairs to see who it was or what they wanted. I came from my hiding spot when I heard Momma walking up the stairs. I stood in my doorway with a dumbfounded look on my face. "You didn't hear me calling your damn name, girl?" "Yes, Ma, I heard you, but I was scared. I thought it was the boys who were shooting last night." "Hell, naw! It was the police. They wanted to ask a few questions to see if we heard or saw anything since we live directly in front of the playground." "Weren't you sitting on the porch last night, Chocolate?" I paused for a while, just looking puzzled. I didn't know if I should tell the truth or tell a lie. But somehow Momma could always tell if I was lying or telling the truth. I inhaled deeply before answering. I dropped my head and said, "Yes," under my breath. "So, did you see anything that could cause trouble around here for us?" "Momma, why are you yelling? Yes, I saw a few of their faces, and I know one of the boys, but I don't want to talk to no police, and I don't want to ever go out of this house." "Child, you don't have to be that scared. Just keep your damn mouth closed and stay off that damn porch." "Yes, ma'am." I turned and went back to my room. I kind of stayed in the house, reading and trying to get ahead of the lessons for the upcoming school year for the remainder of the summer. I only left the house if I absolutely had to. Ant-man and his crew were very dangerous. They were always somewhere, beating somebody up or shooting at people. Good thing! I was lucky enough not to run into him on one of my trips out of the house. I guess those two deaths were enough for one summer because no one else died. They held candlelight vigils for the boys, right at the playground where they were killed. One of the boys was just a teenager. His name was Paul. The other boys from the neighborhood called him P-nut. I didn't know the other guy that was killed. He was from a different neighborhood. Word around the apartments was that it was a drug deal gone bad. I hated senseless crimes. I also didn't understand why people sold drugs, knowing that it would ruin their lives or other people's. Being that I was just a third-grader going to fourth, it was something too complex for me to understand. "But how do you ruin someone else's life just to support your own? Where did these harmful drugs come from, anyway?" I wondered.

Chapter Two

Robbed of My Innocents

Summer was over, and the fourth grade had begun. I was in Mrs. Adams' class. She discovered that I could write poems and other bodies of work that were beyond my years. She took a deep interest in my poems and other writings I did. I loved that she was so friendly and wanted to help me develop my writings in a better way, but I hated talking to her because her breath smelled like horse shit. Some days, she would keep me after school, going over my work and showing me different writing styles. She would always say, "You hang on to these! One day, you'll be a rich lady, Shari." I had no idea what she meant, but I liked the sound of being rich. Anything to get me out the hood was ideal to me. One morning, I entered into class, Mrs. Adams could tell something was wrong because I sat through class without saying a word. I was barely doing my work either. She didn't bother me during class, but as I was packing up to head home when the school bell rang, she stopped me in my tracks. "Shari, what's bothering you?" she asked. I just stood there with my back still turned to her, trying to hide the tears that were welling up in my eyes. "Nothing, Mrs. Adams, I'm fine," I said, still with my back to her. "May I be excused to go home?" "Yes, you may, but if you need anyone to talk to, I'm here to listen." "Thanks, Mrs. Adams," I said as I grabbed the door to exit. I cried on my way home, but I knew I couldn't tell Mrs. Adams what was wrong because she would report it to the authorities. That night, I decided to write about it in the form of a short story, which was the type of writing which Mrs. Adams taught me. That morning upon my arrival, I handed it to Mrs. Adams and told her not to read it until I had left for the day. She didn't do as she was told, unfortunately. In the story, I wrote about how I was assaulted on my porch while I was reading. I sat on the porch most nights to hide from my siblings and Momma. While I was reading, minding my business, a boy named Jack from the apartments across the streets was walking by. He said, "What's up, shorty?" and stopped walking. I spoke back and continued to read. A few minutes later, he came back by and asked what I was reading that had my attention so distracted. I told him the name of the book and kept reading. I could see him walking toward the porch, so I lifted my head. Jack was about 15. He always messed with younger girls, joking and playing with them. I didn't want no parts of that cuz I knew it wasn't right. I closed the book, stood up to try to walk into the house, but Jack pushed me against the wall, covering my mouth. "You better not fucking scream! Who you think you are? Walking around here like you're better than everybody in the hood. All the other lil girls speak and hug me, but you always some damn where reading. What's up with that shit? You ain't better than nobody, bitch!" He then proceeded to rub his hand up my legs. I tried to squirm and move his hand, but he kept going. Tears started to run down my eyes as he said, "I'm not gonna hurt you. I just wanna touch it." As he placed his hands inside my clothes and onto my private area. He penetrated me with his finger, repeatedly moving in and out. He kept asking if I liked it and saying it would be our little secret. I inhaled and kneed him in the nuts, breaking loose and running to the house, screaming and hollering. Mrs. Adams kept me after class, explaining she had to report the incident because it was her duty to do so. I begged her not to because it would cause so many unwanted problems for my family and me. With all the pleading and begging, she still handed my note off to the principal who then called my parents. I sat in the principal's office, being asked a million questions by the guidance counselor and others until I just shut down. They suggested Momma take me to the doctor, and she did. The doctor informed her that there wasn't enough force behind it to cause physical harm but that I should speak with a counselor for my mental health. All I wanted was to forget it happened. I was scared and nervous that Daddy would do something to hurt Jack, which could make his crew come after my daddy. I begged them not to report it to the cops, but Momma said if she didn't, he would do the same or worse to someone else's daughter. "It is either jail or hell!" Daddy said. Momma took me to the police precinct after we left the hospital. It was bad enough that I had to relive the situation when I wrote it the first time. Now here I was, having to write it again with more people in my face, grilling me. On the inside, I was crying and screaming for help, but I tried to sit calmly through the ordeal. They let us go home. I hid in my room, underneath the bed all night. I even skipped dinner, though I loved to eat. I was embarrassed and ashamed. The sound of sirens coming through my window startled me. The police had been riding through the apartments all day looking for Jack. I guessed they found him since the loud, obnoxious sirens were glaring through my window. I was too afraid to come from under the bed to even look out the window. After the sirens came to a halt, I could hear footsteps coming up the stairs. Momma peeked underneath the bed, assuring me that I no longer had to be afraid. "The police have Jack. Chocolate, you don't have to stay under this bed. Come out from under here. Your dad and uncle will protect you, baby! You won't go through this alone. I will be at every hearing. He has to make sure he does some time." "He's only fifteen. It's not like he raped me. He just put his hand in there. How much time you think they gonna give him, Momma? I wish I could move out these stupid apartments!" I yelled, covering my head with the cover. "Well, even at that, I'll push for him to get some time because what he did to you isn't right. If he doesn't get any time, I'll see to it that he pays for this!" Momma said, walking out the room. I didn't want them to hurt Jack, but I knew that whichever way it went, my life had just taken a turn for the worse. Jack was a part of a powerful gang in my neighborhood, so I knew I would always be looking over my shoulders, trying to watch my back. I was so afraid to walk to school alone, just in case his crew was waiting for me. I started tucking a butcher knife in my book bag. If anyone ran up on me, they would get cut the hell up. My life over theirs was how I felt. Three months had passed before we started going to court. The first hearing was reset because his public defender stated she didn't have enough time to review the case. I tried to carry on with my normal day to day activities, but the word was out about what happened to me. Ignorant kids would ask, "Did it hurt? Were you crying?" and shit that really just made me wanna kill them. I remember walking home, it was a few days before we were scheduled to go to court, and Jack's girlfriend walked up behind me. She pushed me to the ground so hard. "Listen, bitch, Jack gonna be a daddy in a minute and if you send him to jail, my child will be without a daddy. I'm not raising this baby on my own! You acting like he stuck his dick in you or something! What he did wasn't hurtful to you. You probably asked for it! So you better go tell them people you lied, and you wanna take back all that shit you said. You understand me, lil girl?" "Listen to me, bitch!" I said as I got up off the ground. "Your baby daddy is a child molester, and I hope you're not having a lil girl cuz he is gonna rape her if he doesn't go to jail." I took off running after I said what I had to say because I knew if Diamond had caught me, she would have beaten my ass. I told Momma what happened, and she called the police. I was so damn tired of seeing the police. I honestly wanted all of this shit to be over with.

Friday had come, and it was time for court. I tried to pretend I was sick so that I wouldn't have to go. Momma dragged my ass out of bed, all the while fussing about why it was so important. In my head, I thought, "Damn! It happened to me, not you. I'm fucking scared." I cried and got dressed. The whole ride, Mommy went on and on about how she hoped they would lock him away forever. I googled such an act, and in my mind, I knew she was hoping for nothing because they weren't going to give him much time. As we got closer to the courthouse, my breathing started to increase as well as my heartbeat. I was scared that if they didn't give him time, he would come do something worse and or kill me. As I sat in court, I could feel the eyes of Jack's gang members and family staring at me as if they were burning through my soul. I was just ready to take the stand so that I could speak my truth and get out of there. The saying that "if looks could kill" was so true at that moment. His mom, Ms. Pam, should be ashamed of herself for wanting her son to get off for this. This grown ass boy molested me, and they were all acting like I was the one in the wrong. As I walked up to take the stand, I could feel my lips trembling and my fingers going numb. I was so nervous, but I knew I had to tell the truth. I took the stand, went under oath, and it seemed as if the questions were never-ending. Jack's lawyer was in for the jugular with her first question. "Explain to me, Ms. Parks, the details of the night in question." With tears in my eyes, I started to explain what happened, exactly how I had written in the letter to Mrs. Adams as well as in my police statement, but this lady was trying to make me out to be a liar. I didn't ask for it nor did I want him to put his dirty, grimy fingers in my stuff! I was just a child, and I didn't deserve what he did to me. After his testimony, the jury went on break for deliberation. His family and mine had to be separated because Momma was talking loud and cursing them out. Court started back shortly, and Jack was sentenced to ten years for child molestation. While I was overjoyed by their decision, I was also terrified about the drama that would unfold between my family and his. The court issued a restraining order to keep him and his family away from mine. They also gave us one against Jack's girlfriend because Momma reported that she was harassing me. It didn't stop her, so eventually her mom was evicted from the apartments, and I didn't see her anymore. As for Jack's family, every now and then, they would say slick shit to me if I saw them in passing, but they didn't cause me any bodily harm. I ignored the threats and their total existence. I tried to bury what happened to me so far in the back of my head, hoping that eventually it would be erased from my memory.

Chapter Three

Strangers turned Friends

A year later, who would have ever thought that I would be sitting in the cafeteria having small talk with a couple of girls? So, here's the story of how three totally different girls became best friends from one small conversation. Redbone, then known as Raven Smith, was new to the school and kind of standoffish at first. Her mom and dad divorced, which caused them to relocate from New York to Atlanta. I had run into Jalisa Brown a few times in the school year, but up until now, I had never held a conversation with her outside of school work. She was just too loud and ghetto all the time for me. The type of attention she drew to herself was startling for an introvert such as myself. As I sat, trying to enjoy my lunch, I heard a voice coming from behind me, "Yo! Today's my first day here. Do yawl have designated seats?" Raven asked. I replied, "Not really! We just sit with our class, no specific seat, though. I sit on this end, so nobody bothers me." "You mind if I sit here?" "Not at all!" It was quiet until Jalisa got out of line with her tray and sat next to Raven. "What's up? I'm Jalisa." "What's up, Jalisa? I'm Shari, and that's miss… up north." "It's Raven. My name is Raven." I think it was at that moment we clicked. I liked that Raven checked me about her name. It was a sign that she wouldn't take no shit. I could tell that we all had something in common, and we would balance one another out, although Jalisa could be a little over the top at times.

From that day forward, we would sit at the opposite end of the table from the other kids each day for breakfast and lunch. Most of our daily talks were about the turmoil within our households, drama from the hood and school work. Although we didn't know one another that well in the beginning, it was like we had been together our whole lives. Our friendship was built solid from that little time we spent together in the cafeteria, and we became very close, almost inseparable. Out of the three of our households, I think I had it the worse at the time. Shit in my house was all bad. School and the girls were all I had to look forward to. After all, it was because of them comforting me that I was able to withstand the shit my momma put me through. Momma would always get drunk and take her marital troubles out on me. Don't get me wrong, Momma wasn't always a drinker and shitty mother.

It wasn't until a cold December night when Momma followed Daddy and his mistress to this fancy restaurant in downtown Atlanta. Daddy had been dating this blond head woman from his workplace for about a year before Momma found out. He oftentimes would miss dinner, and other outings, claiming to be working late or working overtime, occasionally. Some of Momma's friends and other nosy ass people from the hood would tell her about seeing Daddy around town with this other woman. Momma was the type that wasn't into hearsay, she had to find out on her own to believe anything. Daddy pushed Momma's last button when he rushed out the house around two in the afternoon, promising to be back before dinner was served. I guess whatever he had going on was more important than having Christmas dinner with his family because we ate Christmas dinner without Daddy. Following dinner, Momma gave my siblings and me extra TV time since we were on Christmas break. I played with my Gameboy while the younger ones watched Rugrats. Momma had just made us brush our teeth and get into bed when I heard screeching car tires in the parking lot right outside my bedroom window. I looked out the window as I always did, trying to see if it was Daddy's car. It was him. As I gazed out the window, trying to figure out what he was searching for in the back seat of his car, his tall muscular built frame, smooth dark chocolate skin, and small slant eyes emerged from the car with urgency. He came rushing into the house. It was a little after eleven in the night, and as usual, he had flowers and a bullshit excuse to offer Momma. Usually, Momma would behave like a naive good wife and accept Daddy's bullshit. But on that night, she was fed up with his bullshit ass apologies and spoke what was on her mind. That night, they argued for what seemed like forever. I sat in my usual spot and listened to them argue. I could feel the sadness in Momma's voice, and I slowly became angry with Daddy for putting her through so much pain. Daddy was busy trying to sell his lies and empty promises to Momma, but she wasn't listening to it. Daddy stormed out of the house in the middle of the argument when he was backed into a corner and couldn't lie anymore. He claimed the reason for his leaving was because he was too upset to sleep next to Momma. But the truth was he would rather be with that other woman than keep listening to his fed-up wife, demanding that her husband respect her and their marriage. Momma was so upset that she took a bottle of wine from Daddy's personal stash, it was then she had her first drink of alcohol ever. Little did I know that my whole life was about to change in the events to follow over the years to come.

From that Christmas night, the life inside my home was shattered. The conversations between my parents were far and few in between. They barely said a few words to each other. Most of the talks between them were strictly about my siblings and me. I wasn't even sure if they slept in the same bed anymore. Months passed by, and the presence of Daddy was little to none. One night, I snuck down the stairs because I thought I heard a strange noise, but once I reached the third from the last steps, I realized it was Daddy on the couch. I could hear him whispering into his cell phone, but he was speaking so low I was unable to make out the words he was saying. He was begging and pleading with whomever was on the other end of the receiver about something. He hung up and let out a huge sigh. I could tell he was stressed out and overwhelmed about something. So, I walked down the remainder of the stairs so that he would notice me. "Daddy, you scared me. I heard a noise. I thought someone had broken into the house." "No, baby girl! It's just me. You can go back to bed," Daddy said. I replied, "Can we talk for a minute? It's been a while!" "Yeah, sure, princess. What's on your mind?" "I just don't understand what's going on with you and Momma and why yawl must fight so much." Well, baby girl, sometimes adults don't get along, and lately, I have been making a lot of bad decisions. Chocolate, you're too young to understand, so I won't go into details but know your mom and I love each other. We both want what's best for you, your sister and brother." I must admit that talking with Daddy for that short time made me feel a little better. I woke up on the opposite couch from where Daddy was sleeping, and he was gone. Just like that, without a word. I checked the rest of the house to see where the other members of my family were because I was shocked to see that I was able to sleep past nine a.m. Momma was still in bed, and DJ was lying beside her, watching Tom and Jerry on mute. I guess he didn't want to wake Momma. I stuck my head in the door to see if he had eaten anything for breakfast. "Good morning, DJ! Have you eaten this morning?" I asked. He replied, "No! I'm not hungry. Thank you, sister." I smiled and pulled the door back up. I continued down the hall to my sister's room. As I approached the room, I could hear her talking in different voices and trying to speak in different accents. "Shante, are you hungry?" I said as I opened the door to find her playing with Mia, the little girl from next door. "Shante, who let her in here? You know how Momma feels about guests!" "Daddy let her in when he left a few minutes ago. He said we could play tea party." "Well, you know if Momma wakes up, you'll be in big trouble, young lady!" I yelled, closing the door then opening it back up to get her answer as to if she was hungry or not. "Do you want cereal? Yes or no?" "No, Meaney, I don't!" "Fine!" I said, and I stuck my tongue out in a playful manner and closed the door again. I headed backed down the stairs for the kitchen to fix some cereal and call the girls to see if they were awake for our normal morning 3-way call. I would always call Redbone first so that we could talk about Tom and Jerry's love/hate relationship before Jalisa got on the line because she didn't care to talk about a mouse chasing and beating up a silly cat. Once the whole gang was on the line, we immediately started making plans for our day. My momma had become so depressed about her failing marriage that some days, she forgot she had children. So, I knew whatever I was planning, I had to keep Shante and DJ in mind since they would more than likely have to follow up behind me. Some days, I would get frustrated because my fun and play time was limited because they were too small to play and do all the stuff I really wanted to do. The Christmas break was almost over, and I was stuck babysitting the whole time. The last two days of the break, my mom's only sister came into town. She was a shorty stalky, mean, strictly business type of person. She came to take my sister and brother with her for the weekend so that Momma could pull herself together. My aunt tried to encourage my mom to leave Daddy's no-good cheating self. The truth is, no matter the pain and suffering Momma was experiencing, she wasn't ready to leave

Daddy just yet. I enjoyed the last two days of my break, running around the neighborhood with the girls, sitting on the swings, staring up at the stars at the playground that was stationed right in the back of my house.

Sunday came, and the break was officially over. I could smell Sunday dinner brewing in the kitchen. I quickly ran down the stairs, trying to pull my robe on and skip stairs at the same time. I was excited because I thought that Momma was up and feeling better. To my surprise, it was mean ole Aunt Shelly in the kitchen, preparing dinner in Momma's absence. Aunt Shelly was able to get Momma to come out the room and have dinner with us. Just as usual, Daddy didn't show for dinner. But that was no surprise, and it didn't make it better that Aunt Shelly was here because they hated each other's guts. So, I really wasn't expecting him to show. We ate silently, and Momma and Aunt Shelly sat in the living room, eating and talking. I cleaned off the table once we were done, washed the few dishes and put the little ones in bed. I didn't want to disrupt Momma's conversation, so I just did my usual routine.

As I was in the shower shampooing my hair, I could hear loud pitched voices which sounded like it was in distress. I hurried to wash the soap out, but it seemed as if someone was adding more soap because the suds were never ending. Finally, it cleared out, and I jumped out the shower, almost hitting my head on the bathroom sink. I raced to put my clothes on and took the stairs two at a time. I hit the bottom, and I could see Aunt Shelly all up in Daddy's face. He wasn't saying a word. He was just staring at my aunt with a blank expression on his face. Momma sat on the floor near them, begging them to stop fussing before they would wake the other two. The first pause my aunt took, Daddy replied, "Are you done?" Before she could even answer, he was on a rampage about how she needed to mind her own business and stay out of his and Momma's relationship because their marital issues were between the two of them and no one else. My aunt cut in with, "It stopped being between the two of yawl when my sister called me, crying because you don't know how to bring your tired ass home let alone keep your dick in your pants! Now, I'm going to say this, and I'm leaving to go tend to my own marriage, you better start respecting my sister around here. If your trifling ass is out cheating, you'd better not bring her back no sexually transmitted diseases, you nasty ass dog!" Aunt Shelly walked off, slamming the door behind her. Momma still was seated on the floor when Daddy walked past, kicking her out of his pathway as he shoved past me to go up the stairs. I ran to Mama's side, holding her, asking if she was OK. As usual she said, "Yes, baby! Momma is okay. You shouldn't be seeing this. Go to your room, Choc!" I refused to leave her, instead I went into the kitchen to make a homemade ice pack with ice and the bags you get from the grocery store. I handed it to Momma and instructed her to place it on her side so that it wouldn't bruise her. Too ashamed to look me in my face, she grabbed the plastic bag from me without even lifting her head. I sat at the bottom of the stairs, I could hear her praying, and I could also hear Daddy opening and closing drawers in his and Momma's room, which was right above the foyer and the stairs which I sat upon. I encouraged Momma to pick herself up from the floor and move onto the couch. I kissed her forehead and left her there alone. I went into the washroom where there was only a washer and no dryer. I put in a load of clothes so that we would have clean uniforms for the week. Once they were done washing, I hung them around the house to dry. I sat on the edge of my bed, flipping back and forth between Kim possible and power puff Girls. I was trying to figure out if I should call the girls or just keep this to myself. Daddy had never hit Momma, no matter how bad they argued. I didn't see why he should kick her when it was Aunt Shelly that was all in his face. Just like the rest of us, he knew better than to step to her. Her husband was a part of the Mason's and was on active duty in the U.S Army. Had Daddy even raised his hands to her, he would be a dead man. Uncle Reggie which is short for Reginald didn't play when it came to his Shelly. I wished that Momma would be as strong as her sister, maybe we wouldn't be dealing with this crap from Daddy. I refrained from calling the girls because it's too embarrassing to say my father kicked my mother in the side while she just lay there and took it. I wanted so badly for her to stand up to him and demand her self-respect and have some dignity. I had grown tired of hearing Momma cry, so I dressed Shante and DJ, and we went to the park. They loved for me to push them on the swings. I just wanted to keep them happy and unscarred. We played and raced for a few hours. I wanted to make them tired so all I had to do was put them in the shower and then bed. Following their baths, I took one myself. I called the girls but not to talk about what happened; I needed to see what colors we would wear to school. I didn't really sleep well that night. I kept trying to listen out to see if Daddy was coming back home. He never showed up. I was not sure if I should feel good about that or feel sad. Truth be told, I missed him being home, whether he interacted with us or not. It just felt good to have a father living in the house unlike other kids who are raised in their single parent broken homes. I hopped out the bed and went straight to the restroom. I looked at the person looking back at me in the mirror and said, "You are stronger than your circumstances!" I winked at her and grabbed my toothbrush. I brushed my teeth, washed my face, ran my fingers through my hair, and rushed back to the room to get dressed. As I was walking down the hall, past Momma's room, I could hear her talking, but I couldn't make out the words. I wanted so badly to stand there and be nosy, but we were already running a little behind our usual schedule. So, I dressed Shante and DJ as fast as I could, and we were out the house in an instance. Nowadays, what was usually a hot breakfast at the dinner table became waking up extra early to make it to school for breakfast. Lunch was still the same cold cuts. Some days she would be so consumed in her alcohol and sorrows that I would have to end up feeding my siblings and myself. My father's actions caused Momma so much pain that she began to fail us terribly as a parent. All her motherly duties fell upon me now. She no longer had time to help with homework or do the house chores because she was too busy playing private investigator.

Being the oldest of three kids meant that I had to be the caretaker of the younger two. I spent most of my evenings helping Shante and DJ with homework, cleaning the best I could for my age, and ironing school clothes for the next day, instead of playing outside like a normal ten-year-old. Being the person I was, my needs often came last because I was forced to play momma, so I had to do what was best for Shante and DJ. Sometimes the girls would come over and keep me company and help me out a little with completing my homework and other stuff I needed to get done. One Saturday morning, we were sitting on the couch, while Shante and DJ watched cartoons, just having small talk about escaping the hood and having a better life. I told the girls that I wanted to go to college far away so that I didn't have to turn back home. I kind of felt bad because I would have to leave my siblings behind, but I felt like I needed to do what was best for me at some point in my life. I wanted to go to school up north or maybe even in southern California. The girls weren't too pleased with my decisions because it meant that they wouldn't see me either. I tried to convince them to go with me. We all had pretty good grades in school, so I know we could land plenty of scholarships and grants.

They weren't hearing it. Jalisa wanted to stay in the city because she had dreams of a get-rich-quick scheme.

She was going to get a baller and make him her boyfriend and have him buy her a building and open her own bakery. I can't lie, the girl could bake her ass off, and it all started by cooking cookies and cakes in our Easy Bake Ovens that we would get every Christmas. Anytime she had a new idea or recipes, she would come to my house, so we could try it out. Raven's plan was to graduate high school and land a modeling gig. She was enough to do so, and her runway walk was fierce. If that didn't work out, she would go to college to be a pediatrician. We had big dreams and high hopes for ourselves even at a young age.

Later the following year, I graduated from fifth grade. It was the worst day yet; Momma and Daddy argued all the way to the school about who did what and who pushed me the hardest to keep up my straight A grades. Truth be told, neither one of them had been much of a parent throughout most of that academic school year. Daddy was too busy cheating, and Momma was too busy watching him slip in and out of hotels with that home-wrecker. It was because of my own determination and drive that I was able to keep my grades up while trying to care for my sibling best I could. I knew I had to keep good grades if I ever planned on getting out of that hell hole in which we lived. I hated being there. I was glad school was out for summer. I planned on sleeping late and playing with my friends at the park on the daily. I was sadly mistaken if I thought things were going to go that smooth. Drinking had become a norm for Momma. I remember one night, hearing Shante screaming so loud that I thought someone had died in her arms. I ran through the house, trying to figure out where she was and what was wrong with her. As I ran into my mother's room, I saw her face down in her own vomit. I guessed Shante thought she was dead. I woke her up and helped her to the bathroom so that she could gather herself. As I sat outside the bathroom door, I could hear Momma praying and talking to herself. She also informally apologized for the way she had been neglecting us. Once she was all cleaned up, she exited the bathroom, feeling ashamed. She called Shante to the room to apologize to her for what she had seen. Momma felt bad because up until that point, she and I had hidden her drunken behavior from the younger two as best as we could. I actually felt sorry for Momma, but then again, was it even worth all the energy she was giving the situation? I asked myself numerous times, "Why don't you just put him out instead of hurting so bad for the way he's treating you?" I was just a child, so I didn't quite understand love and all that it came with, but I knew Momma didn't deserve what Daddy was doing to her. She was a good woman. Prior to Daddy's cheating and not coming home stunts, Momma would iron his clothes for the workweek, she always had dinner ready when he came home from work, kept the house clean, she would draw his shower water for him, kept herself up and waited on him hand and foot like he was some type of king or something. I kind of looked at her as his slave because I didn't understand why she would do all these things that he was capable of doing for himself. Like couldn't he draw his own shower water? It's not like he was a handicap. He was perfectly able to do all the things she did for him, like turning on the shower himself and fixing his own plate and walking to the table and having a seat. Instead, Momma did everything for him. She called it being a "Good Wife." I called it being a slave. However, I was just a child that didn't know anything about how a "good wife" was supposed to treat her husband.

Another year had passed, and things were still horrible in my home life. It was hard being a mother figure to two kids when I was just a kid myself. My sixth-grade year was kind of a blur. Nothing really exciting happened, and everything was still going the same. Momma was still self-harming by indulging in alcohol to escape the troubles of her failing marriage. I still had to help look after my sister and brother and tell lies to the family about Daddy's whereabouts. I struggled to keep up my grades and meet expectations at school that year because I was so full of anger. The last day of school was the best day of that whole year. Most of the year, I didn't even have enough energy to play and interact with the girls. Don't get me wrong, we had our normal talks in the lunchroom like we had been doing, but I was the one with the juiciest stories, so it left me doing all the talking. Unlike the other kids, I rarely attended field trips or participated in school activities because I had to pick up the younger two. They were very sweet and respectful children just as myself, so I didn't mind looking after them. The school year seemed to be coming to an end faster than I could blink. I hadn't done anything rememberable for the year, so I decided to join a few classmates in a game of truth or dare on the last day of school. During the first round, I was dared to put clear glue all in the seat and up the back of our teacher's chair. So, I did just that! The class could barely keep their composure at the thought of Mrs. Jared not being able to get out of her seat. She was one of those teachers that always had an attitude and didn't like their job, so all the snickering made her upset. Just as she went to stand, she realized she was stuck. Oh, that really pissed her off, she jerked her body hard, and as a result, she ripped her pants! The whole class burst into laughter. Mrs. Jared ran from the class and didn't return. The school was out, and before I knew it, summer had passed me by.

Chapter Four

Hot Stuff

It was the seventh-grade year, and things were off to a good start. Momma slowed down on the drinking and started back doing her motherly duties. I was so stoked about being able to play in the yard with Jalisa and Redbone. Momma was kind of strict, so I couldn't go too far from the front door. If somehow I ventured off further than she preferred, she would stand on the front porch and yell my name until I reached the porch. It was so embarrassing, and the boys in the neighborhood teased me all the time about her doing me like that. It only made me upset because I had a big crush on this one boy who teased me the worse. His name was Marcus Davidson. Marcus was so handsome with his fairly bright skin, medium height, and low temp fade. His mom had a decent job, so she always kept his gear up. He wore his pants slightly down, so you could see his Ralph Lauren underwear. He wasn't arrogant, but he kind of had the big head like he knew he was cute, so he used it to his advantage. At breakfast, he would try to use his charming good looks to get extra food from all the girls in our class. Most times, he could sucker this ugly girl named Jordan into giving him her whole tray. I felt sorry for them because they didn't realize he was running the same game on all of them. He already knew not to come ask my girls and me for our food. Even if we weren't going to eat, we would throw it away before we gave it to his big head self. Although he teased me all the time, I knew he had a crush on me too because he would always play fight with me. One day we were lining up for connections, and he came up behind me, pretending to put me in a chokehold. I could feel him trying to press his penis up against my booty. I yelled and wiggled, trying to break free of his grip, but he was holding on to me so tight. On the inside, I loved every bit of it, but you know, I had to play tough. I fussed and cussed his ass out until he let me go. After we arrived at connections, he had his homeboy, Jarvis, pass me a note. I reluctantly opened the note: "You know I like your short cute ass, so you need to stop playing with a nigga and give me your number." (My response): "You know I've been digging you since the beginning of school, but you're a big flirt and be in all the girls' faces. I don't wanna have to kick your ass." (Passed the note back to Jarvis) I stared him down as he read my reply so that I could see his facial expression as he read the note. (Jarvis as he passed me back the note): "Just write your damn number down. I'm not the fucking mailman." (Me): "Shut the hell up, Jay! It's not like you have some better to do," as I snatched the note. Marcus: "Them other bitches ain't you, baby. I know you felt me press that meat up on your booty, lol, but for real, write your number down, man." (Me): "Honey, barely, lol! But here, call me after school: 4046227907. Don't be calling my momma's house all late either." After Jarvis passed him the note for the last time, he just looked up and smiled at me. I gave him a little smirk like, "Yea, okay."

Soon as the bell rang, I ran to find the girls. I couldn't wait to tell them all about the walk to connections and the note during class.

Upon finding them, I started talking without even speaking. I was so excited such that my mouth was going a hundred miles per hour. "Oh, my gosh! Yawl won't believe who asked for my number!" "Who? Chile? Eric?" Redbone asked. "Hell no! Marcus, girl!" I answered. "Why the hell do you like him so much? He is always somewhere in a trick face that's just gonna cause problems for you," Jalisa said. "And whatever problems come, I can handle them. Damn, Jalisa! It's not like I'm trying to marry the nigga; it's just a crush." I answered. Redbone said, "Right, Jalisa! Just chill! You always jumping the guns." And Jalisa said, "Fuck both of yawl." After lunch, we went on about our day, and I didn't see Marcus no more that day. But later that day, he called the house. We talked for about three hours, mostly just school and stuff going on in the neighborhood. The next day and every day after that, Marcus and his crew sat with me at connections. After a while, he became a bit of a distraction. I didn't know how to tell him that we needed to focus on school instead of talking about a bunch of bullshit and joking for the whole class period. On March 26th, we were sitting in connections just chilling like we normally did; however, it was Marcus' birthday. He had tried to convince me the previous night that I should meet him in the janitor's closet. Unlike some of the girls in our grade, I was still a virgin. As usual, Jarvis passed me a note. It read: "Either we're going in the closet, so you can give me my birthday present or I'll just hook up with Sonia." I wrote back: "If it was that easy, then maybe you should hook up with that bitch and leave me alone. I told you last night I wasn't going in that closet with you, Marcus." Jarvis passed the note to him and back to me rather quickly. I was upset and irritated. Marcus replied, "I really don't want her because she is not finer than you, but the truth be told, if she was my girl, she would be in the closet, serving me up right now. I want yo fine ass to serve me up, not her." I replied, "Marcus, you really got me fucked up! I'm not giving you no head, and I'm most definitely not fucking you in no fucking closet at school!! What the fuck I look like? So, go find you another bitch; I'm done." Jay passed the note back to Marcus, and I told him not to pass it to me no more. I was done with his foolishness. I could see him making that lil face he always made when he's mad, or some shit didn't go his way. I already knew he was about to go off. As I got the note from Jarvis, I said to him, "Man, can you please tell your boy to leave me alone? I'm not his girl no more!" Jarvis said, "Man, I don't have shit to do with that. You tell him." As I read the note, I became infuriated! Marcus called me a bitch and said that he was going to spread a rumor that I gave him head on the playground in the apartments while all his friends watched. I yelled out loud in the class, "You already know when I get home I'ma tell my cousins, and they gonna kick yo ass!" I got up and moved. I didn't say anything else to him for the rest of the day, although he had Jarvis to try and pass me a note. I threw that shit right in the trash. I didn't want to hear his weak-ass apology, because he was only apologizing, knowing my cousins were gonna beat his ass if I told them what he said and planned to do. I didn't even tell the girls what happened at connections this time. I had to sit through lunch with a fake smile and constantly remind myself in my head, not to mention it. I knew if I told them, Jalisa's big mouth ass would make me feel bad about the shit, so I would rather just not mention it. I told Redbone because, unlike Jalisa, she wasn't judgmental and didn't really do the whole "I told you so" thing. After lunch, I was so anxious to get home. I couldn't wait to tell my cousins on Marcus' ass, so they could beat him up. I sat quietly through my last three periods, just waiting for the bell to ring. Soon as that bell rang at 3:45 pm, I ran to the school bus, I didn't even wait for the girls like I usually did. I sat in the seat, anxiously waiting for my stop to come up. On this day, it annoyed me that my stop was the third and last stop. I was just ready to make Marcus eat his disrespectful ass words. Finally, we reached my stop, and I ran off the bus straight to my aunt's house to get my cousins. I could see

Marcus walking all fast, trying to get home. *"There he goes, Quan! There he goes!"* "Now, what's that shit you said in that note, Marcus?" Before he could get any words out, my cousin punched him in the mouth. "Don't ever fix your mouth to disrespect my lil cousin, nigga!" We turned around and walked off. Marcus didn't call me that night like I expected him to, but I didn't care because he was not worth my time anyway. The following morning, I got up, did my normal routine, but Marcus was on my mind. I knew I shouldn't be thinking about him, but I was. I daydreamed about us being in that closet. As we entered, we were kissing, Marcus had his hand twisted around my hair, holding me so tight while he put his tongue down my throat. He pushed me up against the wall as he tried to lift my shirt. I stopped him, asking if it would hurt. He pushed me back against the wall, promising that he would take his time with me. He started kissing from my neck down to my stomach. He looked up at me, unbuttoning my pants, sliding them down to my ankles. He kissed my inner thigh and then slowly started rubbing my clit and blowing on it. The coolness of his breath sent chills up my spine. I breathed in deeply, wishing he would just lick me already. Just as I was looking down at him, he smiled while pushing my legs open. He sucked my clitoris and licked my pussy. My soft moans were now loud, and I felt as though I was about to explode. Then suddenly, I snapped back to reality. Now, here I thought maybe I should have gone into that closet. The afterthought was over, and so was my relationship with Marcus. It had no choice but to be over since my big mouth self-told my cousins about his disrespectful ass. I finished putting my clothes on and hurried out the house before the girls left me with their impatient asses. I was very quiet during breakfast because I was unsure if I had made the right decision. I asked myself over and over in my head if it was really that serious, and if I really wanted to cause harm to Marcus.

In the same instances, it was too late to second-guess things now. As the day progressed, the more shot my nerves became. I was so nervous my hands started to shake. I was dreading running into Marcus. I hoped he had stayed home to avoid the whole ordeal. The ringing of the lunch bell startled me so badly, and I let out a scream. This girl next to me asked if I was okay, and I told her, "Yeah, the bell startled me. I was daydreaming, I guess." I gathered my things and went a different route to lunch than usual, trying to avoid running into him. I sat at the table, fighting to catch my breath as if I had dodged a bullet. I knew that by my nervousness, I would have to tell the girls what was going on because there was no way I could hide this. I didn't even get in line to get my lunch tray. I waited in fear for the girls to come to the table. Jalisa sat down first with her big mouth alley self. "Damn, girl! Why the hell are you sweating so badly? You OK?" "Man, Jalisa, I have something to tell yawl, but we gotta wait until Redbone comes because I don't want to repeat it more than once," I replied. As Redbone came to the table, I took a deep breath because I knew Jalisa's nosy ass would be ready for me to spill the beans before the damn tray hit the table. So, I started with, "OK! So, Marcus and I got into a fight yesterday in connections. Shit went left real fast, and before I knew, I had my cousins involved. Now they are supposed to be coming to the school to fight Marcus. Yawl know I'm scared they gonna hurt him bad then I'ma be sad. I don't really want the stupid fool to get hurt. I just want them to teach him a lesson. Don't be calling nobody's sister/cousin bitches." I was still trying to make sense of my decision when the bell rang for dismissal. I knew my cousins would be out there waiting on the punk ass boy that had to result to name-calling to defeat a girl. I stood in our normal meeting spot, waiting for the other to come. By that time, I had bossed all the way up like, "Shid! Fuck it. It's too late to feel bad now. The show must go on." Just like I thought, Jalisa's big mouth ass came, running, talking about how Marcus called some of his cousins to the school as well. So, now I was pissed off that I even felt bad about what was about to happen to this pussy boy. I walked in the direction Jalisa was going in to see who this nigga had with him. And to my surprise, he had quite a few people standing with him. I whipped out my phone so fast to call and warn my cousins that this nigga brought a crowd with him. If only I had kept my big mouth closed instead of being so quick to holler, "I'ma get my cousins!" they would have caught his ass slipping, but now, it gotta play how it's gonna play out. I stood in front of the stairs where Marcus and his crew were waiting for my posse to show up. Soon as my cousins pulled up five cars deep, I yelled, "Yea! What was all that shit you were talking, lil boy? Call me a bitch while they right here." Just as Marcus was saying, "Fuck you, bitch!" my cousin hit him in the mouth. Everyone was brawling, and I just wished that it was over in my head. It didn't register in my mind that I could get in trouble for having people come to the school to fight. I was just trying to teach this punk a lesson. It's not okay to just walk around, calling females out their name. I also didn't expect them to beat him so badly. I mean, I just wanted them to scare him a little bit. But Marcus had so much mouth, and he wanted to prove a point in front of his friends and shit, so I guessed he kind of got what he deserved. I was not sure why I was sitting there feeling so bad for his ugly ass. Once the fight was broken up, my cousins hopped back in their cars and drove back to the hood. If I was smart, I would've got my bird brain ass in the car too because now, I was sitting in the principal's office, waiting for my parents school was already over for the day. The principal just sat there, twisting back and forth in his rolling chair, not saying a word. Once my mom got there, the receptionist buzzed in the office to let us know. My heart kind of fell into my stomach because I knew Momma was about to be so pissed with me and the poor decisions that I made. Mom sat there, assuring the principal I wasn't raised like this wild, untamed child I was portraying myself to be despite the fact that I was living in a wild jungle. Little did she know my environment was preparing me to be this beast that I was becoming. When it was my turn to speak, I put on my sweet innocent voice and tried to use my smarts and grades as leverage to get me out of this mess. The shit didn't work. I ended up getting suspended for ten days. Marcus was suspended as well for bullying. As we headed home, Daddy stopped at a western union because he claimed he had to send an employee some petty cash until payroll went out. When he got out, my mom called Aunt Shelly, saying she was fed up, and she wasn't going to take this shit from Daddy no more. When she saw Daddy coming out, she hung up the phone in my aunt's face. Daddy hated when Momma discussed their business with Aunt Shelly because she would give him hell about treating her sister the way he did. "Shari!" "Yes, Daddy!" He started with, "Listen, baby! You're too young and too pretty to be fighting about a boy. Your cousins could have been hurt trying to protect you." Just as I was about to respond to Daddy, Momma cut me off. "How the hell you gonna give her a speech about boys?" "Sherry, don't start this shit in front of her! Our business ain't none of her business, and I'm talking to my damn daughter, not you." "Hell! You made it her business a long damn time ago," Momma said. "Chocolate, listen to me, baby, no lil boy deserves that much of your energy. I don't want no lil punk to have that much power over you that he can use words to get you that mad." "Okay, Daddy! You're right, but he said he was gonna say some mean things about me. I don't want people to believe that I'm that type of girl." "See, this is why you're too young to date. Wait until you're older, and you're more mature to deal with this kind of pressure. Dating comes with a lot of ups and downs. You're not ready for that." "Okay, Daddy!" We pulled up to the house, and I went right to my room.

Chapter Five

Price to pay

It was a cool spring night when Momma followed Daddy to the hotel for the last time. Although things were better within my household, Momma was still aware of what was going on with my father. Daddy was still dating the blonde head chick that worked with him. He didn't miss dinner as often, but when he did, Momma knew where he was. Due to his ignorance, he still used the same lie, claiming to be working late or mandatory overtime to cover his behind. Daddy and the blonde head lady checked into their normal room, where they usually met. Momma gave them a while to get into the room and settle down before she would storm in. As she was waiting, the fire within her was raging, and she could no longer wait, wondering what they were in the room doing. At five feet six inches tall, a hundred and thirty pounds Sherry slung the hotel room door open. The blonde head lady was on her knees in front of the chair my daddy was sitting in, giving him head. Mommy damn nearly beat the lady to death before she tied her to the very chair my father was sitting in, getting his dick sucked. Momma poured herself a glass of their wine, walked to the mirror, fixed her hair and reapplied her lipstick. She sat on the dresser in room 112. For a while, Momma just sat there, looking at Daddy and the lady, scared for their life. Momma laughed like a crazy mad woman, sipping the wine she poured herself. After Momma had the third glass of wine, she started questioning Daddy about what was going on. She first started by giving them a couple of rules to the game they were about to play. "Rule number 1. I want to hear nothing but the truth. #2. Speak when spoken to. #3. I want to know the exact places yawl went to, every detail about what and how yawl fucked. . Spare me the lie!" Momma continued, "So, Derrick Sr., where did you meet her?" "We met at a bar one night while I was out with Drew, from across the street," Daddy answered. Momma jumped off the dresser and hit Daddy across the head with the gun she pulled from her purse. She laughed while shaking her head at the lie Daddy told. She waved the gun back and forth while she called Daddy a liar under her breath. Momma continued, "So, you're going to lie to my fucking face, Derrick? I know the fucking truth, so don't try lying to the next question. Let me ask her. Where did yawl meet and what's your name by the way?" "My name is Karen. We met at work. I'm the manager at Stanford Construction Company. Ma'am, please don't kill me. I have a baby at home," the lady answered. "Excuse me, but I'm the only one making demands! You just answer my damn questions. You understand me?" Momma said. "Yes! Yes, I understand," Karen. "Now, Derrick, what attracted you to this bitch, Miss Karen, here?" Momma said, pointing the gun toward Karen. "I don't know, baby! She was just different, and she was there for me when I was about to lose my job three years ago," Daddy said. "Oh, so you were about to lose your dead end ass job, and you fucked the white bitch of a manager of yours to keep that piece of shit job, Derrick? Huh? What is it about this bitch that you were willing to fuck up your family and the life we built?" Momma said. "I don't know, baby! I don't know. I love you, Sherry! I love you, baby. You gotta believe me. I'll let all this go, please. Just don't hurt her anymore. Please, baby, please," Daddy pleaded. "So, you care about this bitch? You bastard. Look what you've done to your fucking family!" Momma said. Then, Karen said, "We are his family too, Sherry. Don't you know that? Derrick, you didn't tell her?" Sherry said, "What the fuck you mean we? Bitch, what makes you family? He hasn't told me what?" Karen responded, "That's right, we, my daughter and I, are a part of his family, just as Sheri, Shante, Derrick Jr. and yourself." Sherry said, "Derrick, what the fuck is this white bitch talking about?" Derrick answered, "Baby, please let me explain!" Sherry yelled, "Fucking explain then, Derrick, I'm listening!" Then Derrick said, "One night, Karen and I met right after work for a quickie. I didn't have a condom, and I didn't have time to stop for one because I had to meet you at the school for DJ right after that. We had been having sex for long, I just thought one time wouldn't hurt. So, we had sex without a condom, but I wasn't thinking about her getting pregnant. However, as it turned out, Karen ended up pregnant, but we weren't sure if Sky was my daughter. We just found out she was my daughter after her first birthday last month." Sherry said, "So, she's not just fucking my husband; she has a fucking baby by him, too." Momma kept repeating that as she walked from the front of the room to the back. She stopped to drain the last of what was left in the wine bottle and sat back on the dresser, looking at Karen and my father. After Momma regained her composure once more, she started asking more questions. Only now she was strictly speaking to Karen. Daddy pleaded in the background for Momma not to hurt them, but she ignored him. "What does she look like?" Momma asked Karen. "She looks just like Derrick, but she has my greenish-brown eyes and curly hair," Karen answered. Momma asked her, "Do you have a picture of her that I can see?" "Yes, in my wallet in my purse. You can get it out if you want," Karen said. Momma sat quietly, looking at the pictures of Sky. Sky reminded her of me, the only difference was that Sky was very light-skinned, and I was a mocha-colored girl. "Karen, I'm going to give you a chance to live to see your daughter grow up. Only because I know how it feels to be a mother and to want to be with your children. But only if you never mention what's about to happen in this room," Momma said. "Sherry, please don't do anything stupid; your children need you. He's not worth you losing your kids and life, is he?" Karen pleaded. "Karen baby, he has already cost me that! I followed you motherfuckers for so long that I missed doing homework with them, playing with them, talking to Sheri about boys, every fucking thing. So, don't tell me about my kids missing me! Hell, my kids hate me because of yawl!" At that moment, it was 3:45 a.m., Momma turned and faced the mirror; she said a prayer, turned back around and shot Daddy in the head. Karen didn't witness his death because Momma thought it was best if she didn't see it; she had tortured her enough. Momma had her blindfolded the whole time. Momma hit Karen in the head with the butt of her pistol before leaving the hotel room that night, leaving Daddy and Karen tied to the chairs. They both bled like crazy. Once Karen came back conscious, she tried screaming, but she couldn't find enough strength to do so. Finally, a housekeeper found them. Karen begged her to take her blindfold off and call 911. The housekeeper called the police and checked the room to see if anyone else was there and hurt. She took the blindfold off and untied Karen. The police arrived and immediately started questioning Karen as to what happened in room 112. Too scared to mention Momma being present, Karen acted like she didn't know who entered the room and did this to them. She told the police and detectives that she was knocked out and blindfolded by the intruders upon entry into the room. Being that Karen couldn't provide the investigators with much information, and the hotel company didn't have working surveillance cameras, the police never found out what happened to my father in that room that night. Momma allowed Karen and her daughter to attend Daddy's wake at a specific time but not the funeral because she didn't want people to speculate or gossip. She felt as if she was nice enough to even allow her to see him at all. After all, she was his mistress. Once the funeral was over, and all the phone calls stopped, and people stopped coming by "just to check on us," Momma allowed us to formally meet Sky. She reminded me so much of myself, but I couldn't allow myself to get close to her. She was the reason my father was no longer here. No girl should have to grow up without her father. It was hard for me to digest that I had lost my father and gained another sister in the same instance. I had a lot of built-up anger about my father's death and him having a child with another woman, but I had to pretend that I wasn't bothered on the surface because someone had to be strong for DJ and Shante. Dealing with the death of my father drove Sherry back to drinking on a regular basis again. I guessed it was eating her up, knowing she was the cause of her own sorrow. His death took a big toll on DJ and Shante as well. I mean, constantly crying and questioning God on why Daddy had to die. To them, he was their hero. They were too young to understand what was going on and what wrong he had done. I would sit up most nights crying and asking myself why the hell Daddy had to sleep with that bitch and have a baby with her. "What made her so special or better than Momma?" Then I thought, "Maybe he just stopped loving Momma and us, too, but how could he not love his own family?"

Shortly after Daddy's death, DJ started acting out in school and at home. Whenever he was in trouble, he would blame his misbehavior on Daddy being dead and leaving him to act as the man of the house. Due to his behavior, we ended up going to a therapist once a week to talk about our feelings. The therapist would ask personal questions about how things were before

Daddy's death, and I often would just be quiet listening to DJ and Shante tell these stories about things I didn't remember. It just made me angrier. They painted this lovely picture of him that wasn't true. Daddy had been cheating, beating on Momma from time to time and left Momma to care for us on her own. He wasn't there to help with homework, read us bedtime stories, or teach us how to ride a bike. He was not as good a father as they made him out to be for some time now, and that just made me madder. I just wanted them to know the truth about their father, our father, but they were too young to understand. Instead of talking to our therapist, I chose to write in my journal because this family affair was way too personal to tell some lady that didn't know my family. If I chose to talk to her, that would ultimately land my mother in prison, and we would be without two parents. Eventually, I stopped going to the therapy sessions because it was pointless for me. I could see a change in Shante's behavior, but that junior, on the other hand, was a different story. He started hanging with the neighbor's son that was a known badass, and he just made DJ even worse. They would play knock, knock zoom on the older people at the front, of the apartment complex doors and stand at the main street throwing rocks at the cars as they drove by. Momma was so confused as to what to do with him and his behavior, and it made her self-inflicted depression worse. I would try to talk to him and try to get him to redirect his anger, but it seemed like I wasn't getting through to him either. When Momma would fuss or try to whoop him, he would stand in the hall and wish that she was dead instead of Daddy. Little did his badass know that Momma was the better parent. Our father had checked out on our family and started a new family. He didn't give a fuck about us because if he had, we wouldn't be in the situation we're in. Mommy tried to get her brother to help her with DJ. She even signed him up for the big brother program at school because she refused to let him end up a product of his environment. With the help of positive role models, Momma was sure that it would change Junior's behavior and help him to re-channel his anger and aggression. Although he would have some bad days, DJ's overall behavior was improving. DJ was doing better at school, too, since they put him in the behavior class. He didn't have his lil friends with him egging his ignorance on. Being that he was in a smaller class setting, his grades started to improve, and he wasn't walking out the school when he felt like it. It seemed like the year went by rather quickly because before I knew it, the seventh-grade year had come and gone.

It was the first day of summer, and all I wanted to do was hit the park and chill with my girls. I washed my face and threw on a tank top with some leggings ready to jet out the house. But it seemed like the forces of the world were against that. As I got to the steps in front of Redbone's house, her nosey ass neighbor said they had just left. She went on to inform me that I probably wouldn't be seeing her because she was grounded. I said, "OK!" and headed toward Jalisa's house, thinking of what Miss Goody Goody could have done to be grounded. Out of breath, I knocked on Jalisa's door, and her mom was like she couldn't come out. That I should come back later. "Now, who the hell am I supposed to sit at the park with to watch the boys play ball?" Disappointedly, I walked back to the house. "Choc, who pissed in your cereal this morning?" Momma asked. "Nobody. Redbone grounded, and Jalisa can't come outside right now. I'm bored and want to go to the park," I answered. "If you that damn bored, pick up a broom or mop and clean this damn house. That'll give you something to do!" Momma said. "Really, Ma, it's the summertime," I said. "What the hell summer has to do with this house getting cleaned?" she yelled. "Ugh, OK!" I said. I cleaned the downstairs up quickly, grabbed the cordless phone off the wall and headed up for my room. I called Lee-Lee. "Jalisa, why your mom tripping about you coming outside?" "Man, you know she be on some other shit, man. I'ma just wait until she starts drinking later, then I'll ask her if I can come out," Jalisa said. "Okay, cuz you know I'm not trying to be stuck in this house. She already made me clean up the whole damn downstairs." "! Have you seen Raven?" Jalisa asked. "I called her, and her mom said she couldn't talk on the phone. Naw, but I went to her house before I came to yours and her nosey ass neighbor said she was grounded. Man, that broad Ms. Ellis be in every damn body business! All she does is sit on that damn porch or be looking out her bedroom window." "For real, with her police ass. Oh, look, Choc, do you know Austin from Parkway?" Jalisa asked. "Yea! I heard his name before, but what about him, Lee?" "I been talking to him on my Bebo page. He gonna have his big cousin bring him to the apartments later tonight. I need to use you as my alibi. You know Tasha doesn't let me be outside late. At least, if we are at your house, Ma Sherry will let us sit on the playground." "Alright, cool! I'ma clean the rest of the house, so she'll let me have company. Talk to you later," Choc said. "Later!" replied Jalisa. We hung up, and I went to Momma's room so I could try to suck up to her. I lay at the foot of her bed and cut right to the chase. "Ma, you mind if Lee-Lee comes over for the night?" "Choc, I really don't wanna be bothered, but long as y'all stay out my damn way, I don't care. Now get out my room cuz I know that's all you wanted," Momma replied. "Thanks, Ma!" I kissed her forehead and ran to call Jalisa back. "My momma said yea, so, bitch, we on." I cleaned my room and sat in the house, watching the clock, wishing time would go faster. I was bored out my mind and wasn't shit on TV. While waiting on time to pass, I ended up falling asleep. I heard Momma yelling my name, so I jumped up and ran downstairs. "Yes!" "Ms.

Tasha and Jalisa were at the door." "Hey, Ms. Tasha! Hey, Lee!"
"I'ma let her stay the night, but y'all ass better not be up to no
sneaky shit, like sneaking out the house cuz I heard about Raven,
and I told your mom about it too." I was in disbelief that Redbone
had done some shit like that and didn't tell us. In my mind, I was
trying to figure out why the hell she would be sneaking out the
house. "Oh no, ma'am, we not!" I assured her. "Okay, see you
later, Lee-Lee. Don't give Sherry no hard time!" Ms. Tasha said.
"Okay, Momma. Love you!" We closed the door and ran upstairs.
After it started getting dark, we called Austin to see if he was still
coming through. He said he was waiting for his big cousin Offset
to pull up. About forty-five minutes later, he called the phone
back. I was scared because Momma didn't like lil boys calling her
house. I whispered to Jalisa to tell him he couldn't call the phone
back. "Listen, Austin, my auntie doesn't like us giving her number
out, so we just gonna be on the playground waiting for you. When
you get out here, pull into the third parking lot; it's the last
building on the right. Walk to the back, and you'll see the
playground. We either gonna be right there or on Chocolate's
porch." "Alright!" We looked in the mirror to check what we
looked like and went on the back porch. Austin and Offset pulled
up, and we chilled for like three hours. Lee-Lee and Austin were
all over each other, kissing and feeling all on each other. Hell, if
you could get pregnant from kissing and hunching, she would
damn sho be pregnant! Offset was trying to make passes at me, but
he was way too damn old. I did let him spend like fifteen dollars
on snacks and shit from the candy lady. But Offset was in the 12th
grade. I knew he was doing shit I wasn't ready for. I didn't see no
harm in spending his money. Since most of the night, all he talked
about was how much bread he got and how he spoiled all his girls.
Hell, I thought about how I could get him to spend some more on
me in the time we were together, Lee-Lee and Austin were too

busy dry fucking. Right when I was about to make a suggestion, offset got a call on his Nextel and had to leave in a hurry. Austin was gonna stay a lil while longer, but Offset didn't know if he would make it back before we had to go in the house, so Jalisa kissed Austin good night and told him to call her when he got home. We sat on the porch, listening to music and talking until Momma called us in. The next day, we walked to Redbone house to try our luck on seeing if she could come out. Ms. Lisa said that Redbone was starting to smell herself and that we should not be hanging with her. But that was our sister, and it wasn't no trading! We begged and pleaded until finally, Ms. Lisa let her come out. "Bitch, you got some explanation to make," we both said at the same time. "Man, I know damn. Let's just walk away from the damn door cuz I can bet Ms. Ellis' old ass sitting in her window, trying to hear what the fuck we saying." We walked toward my house to the playground. "Okay, so I met this boy like three weeks ago while I was at my cousin, Kim's house. His name is Eric, and he's in the 10th grade. I didn't give him my number or nothing before I left, so I don't know how he got the shit." Kim swore she didn't give it to him, but I knew the bitch was lying. "But anyway, he was whipping different cars, and he pulled up on me like, 'Let's go get some food.' I told him I couldn't cuz my momma would be home from work soon. He promised me that we would be back in time. I didn't know the damn car was stolen, so we went to Red Lobster to get the food we ordered. When we got there, we had to wait like ten minutes, then finally we got the food and walked out to go. We planned to park somewhere to eat and talk. As we walked out, there were police everywhere, so he told me to walk to some apartments next to it and ask somebody to use their phone. He handed me a card and started running. I called the girl whose card he gave me. He said she was his sister and asked her to come get us. I was scared as fuck, man. The whole time, he hid in the bushes. Once the girl got there, we got in the car, and he took me home. I was mad as fuck. I sat at the table, thinking like, 'What the hell did I get into?' After I ate, I took the food bag to the trash so Momma wouldn't see it. I took a shower quickly and put some nightclothes on, trying to pretend I had been home all day. Before Momma could get to the damn door, I overheard Ms. Ellis' fat old ass telling her she needed to watch my fast tail ass. So, Momma said, 'What makes you call her fast? She is not like these lil girls around here.' Ms. Ellis said, 'Shit yes hell she is riding round in cars with older boys.' Momma was like, 'Nah, you got my baby confused.' And walked into the house. So when she put her bags down, she called me downstairs like, 'Where the fuck have you been?' I lied and said I hadn't been out the house. Then she hit m me like, 'Lying ass heifer, that old lady ain't gonna lie on you! If yo fast tail ass wanna be sneaking out the house while I'm not home, you'll spend the summer with yo grandma cuz I don't have time for this shit.' 'Ma, I swear, Ms. Ellis is lying. I been in the house.' 'Yo ass got one more time to do some, and you'll be back up North for the summer, away from yo lil friends and all other distractions.' So y'all, I'm trying to stay out of trouble cuz I'm not trying to go back up there. I told Eric he was trouble, and I couldn't kick it with him, or my mom gonna send me back to New York. This nigga said, 'I'm a scammer, baby. I'll just fly up there to see you.' I don't know what I'ma do with him. I gotta break that shit off by the time summer is over." Man, if I was the one, I'd have taken all his money, but we all know you're too nice for that," Lee-Lee said. "Shut up!" (Laughter!) "We can't all be a savage like you, Lee-Lee." Redbone took all the gifts Eric gave her, but somehow, she managed to do so without Ms. Ellis' nosey ass all up in her business. Oh, and she managed to break it off with Eric before school started. Jalisa's sneaky ass was able to stay low-key, as far as I know. Jalisa and I didn't see Austin nor Offset no more that summer. I'm unsure what happened between Austin and Lee-Lee, but after that night, she didn't mention him anymore. Summer was over, and we all managed to keep our V-cards and stayed out of trouble as far as I knew.

Chapter Six

Final Chapter of Middle School

It was the first day of school, and I was searching high and low for Jalisa and Redbone, but they were nowhere to be found. I dragged myself around the school all day like a sad puppy. Being in school without the girls was sad and depressing. School days weren't fun without the girls. Hell, they were the main reason I was excited about going back to school in the first place. I didn't have anyone to converse with besides Marcus. He had been checking on me daily since my father passed. Somehow, we were able to get over the whole fight situation and just be cool. I was glad that beef was over, and I appreciated him checking on me and helping me cope with the loss of my father. The school day had come to an end. I had never been so excited to go home from school until that day. All I wanted to do was go home so I could start all over again, hoping to see the girls tomorrow at school. That night, I rushed through chores and dinner. I showered and brushed my teeth without Momma having to tell me to do so. By the time she did her usual call out of our names from her bedroom, I was already prepared for bed. That morning I was the first to get dressed for school. I was so amped to see the girls. Little did I know the day would be the same as the previous day. The girls weren't present at school for the second day. I was worried because no matter what, we never missed school. I constantly checked my Mickey Mouse watch, waiting for three forty five to come so I could get home. Finally, I checked my watch for what seemed like the thousandth time, and it was time to go home. Upon my arrival at home, I walked to Shante and DJ's school to get them from the after-school program. I sat in the house and called every number I had for Jalisa and Raven. The only information I received from Jalisa's mom was that she was on punishment for a month. She asked me not to call or come by the house until then. Raven's mom simply told me to stay away from her because she would be a bad influence on my life. I was trying to figure out what the hell they had done that was so bad. I was driving myself crazy, thinking about the girls. I couldn't understand why they weren't attending school or found a way to call me while their moms were at work. They had to know I was worried sick, or did they care I started to worry? Neither Jalisa nor Raven came to school the whole first week of school. I was forced to sit alone in the café, with no one to talk to. The finest boy in eighth grade was having a party for his birthday. I was so pissed that I would miss it because despite the love I had for Marcus, I had a huge crush on Jamal Davis, JD. He was super fine, tall, light-skinned, greenish-brown cat eyes, good curly hair and a body to die for. He played sports for the school and Rec center. All the chicks in school wanted to date JD, but he always acted like he wasn't interested. He was into older girls because they were already having sex. Although I knew I didn't have a chance with mister JD, I still liked him. Hell, at one point, I even thought about giving up the panties just to get him. If I did, it would mean I was the first girl in junior high to get with the infamous Jamal "JD" Davis. However, being that I was taking sex education, I knew sex wasn't an option because I was too scared it would hurt, or I would end up pregnant. On top of all that, JD didn't deserve to have me. I was special and wanted to save myself for as long as I could, plus I would give Marcus some before him. Well, here it was Saturday night, and I was sitting in the house, bored out my mind, watching my sibling play the Nintendo 64. At about nine forty-five, I called Jalisa because I knew her mother was at work. She worked the graveyard shift. Jalisa told me she would sneak out because she knew how much going to this party meant to me. I quickly got dressed and ran out the house and threw the cut to Jalisa's house. Once I got there, she forwarded her house calls to my cell phone in case her momma called to check on her. As we walked, she made me promise not to mention what she was about to tell me. My best friend poured her heart out to me about the hardships her mom was experiencing. Jalisa's mom was struggling to pay the bills because she lost her second job at the nursing home. She worked two jobs so that she could afford the hottest new shit that Jalisa just had to have and to keep her nails and hair done every two weeks. It turned out that Jalisa and Raven had been stealing from all the local malls for about three/four weeks. Just like they had done every day. Jalisa and Raven went to the mall with the biggest handbags they owned. They laughed and joked while searching each rack. Once they had all the items they wanted, they headed for the dressing room. They would quickly took all the sensors off the clothes and stuff all they could into their purse. Then they would pretend to try on outfits, knowing they weren't going to buy anything, but they needed a cover-up. After they pretended to not like any of the stuff, they took the stuff back to the racks. Just as they were leaving the store, the clerk noticed Raven had on a pair of their shades, instead of her notifying them, she called security. Right when they were headed out the mall, the police were behind them. It was then Raven noticed she forgot to take the shades off her head. Police said, "Excuse me, young ladies! I need for you ladies to turn around." Raven replied, "Oh, my gosh! Sir, what's the problem?" "You were caught stealing those shades from a department store."

(Raven felt the top of her head.) "I'm so sorry, sir! I honestly forgot they were up there. I had no intentions of stealing them." "Ma'am, I believe you, but unfortunately, you left the store and was about to leave the mall, which makes it stealing. So, I'm going to have to take you to the security booth and call your parents." "Sir, is that necessary? Can I just take the shades back to the store? I honestly forgot that they were on my head." "I do apologize, but it's store policies, which I must abide by." "Jalisa, go get my mom, please!! Hurry up!" "No, ma'am, she's going to the security booth with you. I can call your parents to pick you up once we are in the booth," the police officer insisted. Jalisa said, "What? Why? I got to go! What I do?" "You were with her, so we must take you in too." "This is bullshit! I didn't do anything; why the hell I gotta be taken in?" "Ma'am, watch your mouth! the officer cautioned. No fuck that! That's not right!". "Yawl bullshit ass police always fucking with people," Jalisa retorted. Raven yelled, "Fuck, Jalisa, chill! Stop cursing! You making the shit worse than it is!" Jalisa shot back, "Fuck you, bitch! How the fuck yo stupid ass forgot to take them ugly ass shade off?" The police officer said, "Both of you don't say another word!" Raven said, Fuck you, bitch." "Fuck, I made a mistake! It was a damn mistake, Lee-Lee!"

Well, as a result, they got to the booth. The store people wanted to let them go, but the security insisted that they press charges for the shades. Being that they were minors, they were sent home, and Raven's mom had to pay for the shades. Out of all the thoughts and scenarios on what they could be in trouble for, this never crossed my mind. I never expected Jalisa's mom to be in any kind of financial hardship. We continued to talk until we reached JD's house. On the porch, we read a note which read: "If you are lame, and I don't fuck with you, don't bother to come in!" I looked at Jalisa, busted out laughing and went into the house. We greeted everybody and talked to a couple of people we knew. There were a lot of girls there who were older than we were, so I figured they were some of JD's whores from high school. As it turned out, they were. The three girls in the living room were friends of the biggest hoe at Weber High, Jennifer Tate. I idealized Jenn because she had the one thing I would love to have, Jamal Davis. Jennifer was about five feet seven inches, light skin, long pretty hair, and banging ass shape. She had slept with most of the boys in both the junior and senior high. See, Jenn lacked everything I possessed, high self-esteem, self-love and self-respect! I stared at her and JD in the kitchen laughing and playing, while sipping out their red plastic cups. Jalisa and I proceeded to walk through the kitchen to the outside because I was desperate to get JD's attention. Just as I had made it one step away from where Jenn and JD stood, they burst into laughter. I could hear Jenn saying, "Look at simple little Sheri." JD replied, "Yeah, look at her hell. She would be fine if she was all grown up like you baby," as he rubbed down Jennifer's hip and leg. I was so embarrassed I took off running. You would have thought I was a track star the way I took off. It took Jalisa a minute just to catch up with me. "Sheri, what the hell is your problem? Why did you run off like that?" "I don't know why the hell I ran, Jalisa. Hell, I was embarrassed, humiliated. I had to get the hell out of there before I kill that bitch, Jenn." "Hell, Sheri, you should have slapped her ass in the mouth for trying to pull your card like that. Now people gonna think you are scared or some shit, Choc!" "Fuck that! Let's go back. I'm not scared of no bitch, and you know that, Jalisa!" "I know, Chocolate, but you gotta prove that to her or she gonna keep trying you. You have let her slide twice already." "You're right! I should have beaten her ass at the park that day for stepping on my forces! Fuck it! I'm going back."

Once we were back at the house, I looked in every room downstairs for Jenn. She was nowhere to be found. I knew she was still there somewhere because her ugly ass friends were still there. So, I went upstairs. Just as I suspected, Jennifer and JD were upstairs having sex. I stood at the door, listening to her moan and the loud echo of smacking noise like he was slapping her ass. Hearing her yell out his name and calling him daddy made me even madder. I busted into the room. They looked back, and JD smiled and kept hitting Jenn from the back like I wasn't even standing there. They continued like they were putting on a show for me. She moaned and called his name like they were the only ones there. By this time, I looked back and noticed a crowd of people behind me. As I walked further into the room, my pulse started to race, and my body was getting warm from the rage I was feeling. I could hear cameras snapping pictures and voices in the hall instructing me on what to do. Some people cheered me on to join them, but I wasn't about to lose my virginity to this piece of shit, and Jenn surely wasn't about to taste this pussy. Before I knew it, I snatched Jenn right from JD's grip. I dragged her downstairs by her hair. He jumped out the bed, searching for his clothes and yelling for me to let his bitch go. She was yelling, calling me all kinds of bitches and whores, begging me to let her go. I really didn't want to disrespect JD's mom's house, so I let her go and told her to meet me outside. Jennifer wasn't a fighter because she was too scared to fuck up her pretty face. However, that night, she had a point to prove. Just as I had. She wasn't about to let a girl from junior high kick her ass in front of all her people and JD. As she walked out of JD's front door with the rest of the crowd from inside the house, I punched her before she could step off the porch. She fell to the ground, and I was about to step over her, so I could keep punching her, she kicked me. I stumbled, trying to keep my balance. Jenn jumped up so fast. I had to gain my composure before I charged at her again. I hit her about four times before people started trying to grab us and break up the fight. I had my head down because Jennifer was holding my hair and wouldn't let go, so I kept punching her while the crowd was yelling for her to let my hair go. Finally, she let my hair go. JD had Jenn, and Jarvis Grant, Marcus' old friend, and Jalisa had me. I yelled to Jenn, "If you ever disrespect me, I'll beat your ass again, bitch! You leaking! You might wanna get a mirror and check your face!" I was so upset. I still wanted to fight, but Jalisa kept telling me to chill because I had beaten her badly enough. Jarvis offered to walk us home to make sure we got there safely. I had never really paid attention to how cute Jarvis was until that night. He was so strong. He picked my small framed body up and carried me from in front of JD's door, so I could cool off. We talked as we walked. "Chocolate, you are pretty. You shouldn't listen to Jennifer. She's just jealous because you're fine without all that ass she got." We all laughed, and Jalisa and I gave each other that look. "Thanks, Jarvis, that's sweet." "I'm serious, Sheri, you fine and smart. All that makes you better than her because all she has to offer is her body because she isn't smart like you. You don't have to use your body to get people to like you, as she does," Jarvis advised. "I know, Jarvis, but I have the biggest crush on JD." "Damn! Well, too bad! I was hoping you were digging me, Choc." "I'm sorry, J. I mean you cool, but I never really looked at you in that way. You used to be cool with Marcus. Don't get me wrong, you're fine as hell and yo skinny ass strong." (I gave him a playful shove, and we both laughed.) "I understand, Choc, but that was puppy love. I always thought you were too good for that nigga, anyway. He didn't know what to do with you. I know how to treat a girl like you. Watch, you'll be my girl one day." I smiled and lowered my head, thinking about what he said. After that, we all kind of walked in silence the rest of the way. Since Jalisa's house was the first stop, we stopped there first. The rest of the short distance to my house was awkward. We just walked in silence, but I watched the ground as I walked, thinking I could see Jarvis glance at me every few steps. Once we reached my porch, we said goodnight to each other and kissed Jarvis' cheek and ran into the house. I watched Jarvis walk off from my bedroom window. I kind of felt bad about letting him down. "Aye, J!" "Yeah, Chocolate?" "I'm sorry if I hurt your ego, see you in school on Monday," I told him. "It's cool, Sheri. No love lost, baby girl! See you Monday. Remember what I said, though." I smiled. "Cool!" I said and walked away from the window. As I lay in bed, I realized that it was more than just good looks. I figured that I liked JD for all the wrong reasons. Jarvis had opened my young eyes to a new world. It was the world of Chocolate. The new Chocolate, that is. I had to be respected, or that was your ass. I would fight about my respect. Being that almost all the girls were afraid of me after I had beaten Jenn up, I had no worries with being disrespected by the girls. The boys, on the other hand, were a different story. JD and his crew had it out for me since I had beaten up Jennifer. Every day after school, they would threaten me, saying shit like I better watch my back because Jennifer's cousins would be down here in two weeks for her birthday, and they were going to jump me. One day, JD took it way too far. He walked up behind me, grabbed my hair and whispered in my ear, "You fucked with the wrong bitch when you fucked with my bitch!" As he was letting me go, he shoved my head, causing me to fall to the ground. His crew thought it was funny, not knowing how badly I was hurt. Once I got up, they saw blood gushing from my left kneecap; they all ran. I didn't know if I was more pissed at the fact that he had fucked up my brand new seven jeans or the fact that my knee was busted. I had to ride the school bus with blood running down my leg like water. Good thing, I no longer had to pick Shante and Derrick up from school. They were finally old enough to walk themselves home. When I walked in, I was afraid to call my mom because I knew she was going to be mad if she had to leave work. Reluctantly, I called anyway. "Hey, Momma!" "Hey, Chocolate. What's up, baby?" "Momma, don't be mad, but today in school, this boy named Jamal pushed me down and busted my knee cap." "What the hell, Choc? I was down here at Jill's, drinking with San since I had an early release at work. Fuck, you gonna get enough of playing with them lil stinking ass boys! I should let yo ass sit there bleeding. Here I come, damn!" "Ma, I wasn't playing with him. I was walking to get on the school bus, and he grabbed me by my hair!" By the time I finished everything I had to say, she had already hung up in my face. While I was sitting there waiting for Momma to get home, I thought of a plan to teach JD's ass a lesson. I called my most favorite two cousins, Quan and Keem. I told them all about what JD and his boys had been doing to me. I kind of over-exaggerated the situation, but I didn't give a damn because he needed to pay for what he did. Right when I was about to call, Redbone's Momma walked in, so I hung the phone up in a hurry. I didn't want to piss her off worse than she already was since I made her leave from hanging with her girl. She just stood in the doorway, not saying a word. It was like she was shocked. I have never really seen a more scared look than that. Looking at all the blood coming from my knee made Momma go back to room 112. I called her name, making her snap out of her daze. "Damn, baby, I didn't know it was that bad! Come on, let me help you to the car. DJ, grab a towel for your sister for Momma." Once I was in the car, Momma walked next door to ask nosy ass Mrs. Rose to sit with Shante and DJ. Momma didn't say a word the whole ride to the hospital. I thought because I was bleeding, it would speed things up, but boy, I was wrong. That slow ass hospital took forever to call my name just to get a bed. Finally, after I got to the back in a room, they gave me a shot with some pain medicine and a local anesthetic so that they could staple my knee back together. They told me to stay off my leg for two weeks to prevent the staples from coming out. On the way home, Momma hit me with the girl talk. "Sheri, I know you're getting older and starting to like little boys, but I'ma tell you one thing, baby. Never let a man hit you or call you out your name." "Yes, ma'am." "Once you allow a man to start disrespecting you, he'll think it's okay for him to, and it's not. Who is this little boy that pushed you?" "His name is JD, Momma, and I don't like him. I don't know why he and his friends are always messing with me." Okay, so I lied. I did know why JD wanted me hurt, but I couldn't tell Momma I snuck to a party and got into a fistfight with some chick from high school. "Okay, baby, I believe you. I'ma file some charges on that lil bastard if he doesn't keep his hands off you. You're too damn pretty to be letting some knucklehead little boy mess up your body, you hear me?" "Yes, Momma!" "When I say mess up, Choc, I mean that in every way, you know?" "Yes." "So, before you think about sex, you think about what it'll do to your body." "Eww, Momma! I don't wanna have sex no time soon." "I'm just saying, Sheri! Sex comes with a lot of consequences, and I'm not just referring to babies." "Yes, Momma, I understand." "Good! So when you think you are ready, promise you'll come talk to me before you do it." "I promise, Momma!" At that moment, I felt good. Listening to Momma talk like that brought back memories of the good days before she was introduced to alcohol. She used to be so sweet and caring. Besides her fussing about our rooms being dirty or our toys being all over the front room, Momma never really raised her voice back then. In a way, I kind of needed that talk with Momma because we hadn't had a real mother/daughter talk in a while. That short talk on the way home opened a new door of understanding between Momma and me. From that day forward, whenever she was home, she would make small talk with me about boys, school, and about how Shante and DJ were doing in school and stuff. It felt like she was becoming her old self again. I noticed she had stopped drinking so much and going out with Ms. San ghetto ass. Things were going good at 213 Smith Blvd. These new changes brought so much happiness in our house. Shante and DJ were so happy that Momma was in a better space. The vibes in the house were so soothing and calm. Jalisa's house was a different story.

Chapter Seven

Drugs, Traffic, & Money

One day, while sitting in the cafeteria, Jalisa started telling Redbone, Jarvis, and me about her mom's new boyfriend. In doing so, she didn't have anything pleasant to say about this new-found guy. Based on Jalisa's thoughts and the images she painted for us, this was not the type of man you would want to be around your child. So, Momma had been seeing this dude named Black from the Ward. He's supposed to be some big-time drug dealer round that way. Momma met him at the blue store when she went to play her numbers. He was flashing his money and giving orders to all the young boys, so the flashy shit caught Momma's attention. The first day they met, they ended up going out later that night. Black gave Momma like three stacks and told her to treat herself to something nice. They would meet almost every other night right up at the motel by the apartments. I couldn't figure out where Momma was getting all the money from, all I knew was that we weren't struggling no more, and Momma was all happy and shit. Black got tired of meeting at the motel and just moved himself into our apartment. Eventually, he made our apartment into the trap spot and was selling drugs and hoes out our house. Man, all his little workers would be at the house all night. All they did was talk shit, play music, play cards, and run in and out all night. I barely got any sleep. Some nights, I was unable to do my homework. It was so loud I couldn't concentrate. "Jalisa, you know, my momma has cut back on the alcohol, so I can talk to her to see if you can stay at the house for a few days, so you can get some sleep," I said. "Thanks, Choc! I really need it. I appreciate you offering me your house, girl. I promise you, sometimes I would be afraid to go to sleep, thinking somebody gonna come into my room." "Choc, if any of them niggas touches you, I have some people that I can send their way. You know I'll always protect the three amigos," Jarvis said. (We all burst into laughter). "Thanks, Jarvis! I know you will. That's why I love yawl so much. Yawl always have my back. You know Tasha Brown ain't about to let me leave her house. I wish I could because Black scares me sometimes too. He always wanna hug me. And he licks his lips when he talks to me. One day, I was cooking in the kitchen. He told me to holler at him when I was ready to be a woman and keep a bankroll. Whatever the fuck that's supposed to mean. I told Momma, but she said he was just putting me up on the game," Jalisa narrated. "I'm telling you, Jalisa, you need to let me send my people to The Ward to holler at him, just so neither he nor anyone in his crew ever thinks about harming you." "No, J! It's cool, really! You know I can't let you put your life on the line like that. I can handle this myself, but I promise to let yawl know if shit gets any worse." "Okay, Jalisa, because you know yawl have become like sisters to me. It's my brotherly instincts to look after yawl. Plus, if anything happens to yawl, Choc gonna go crazy." Chocolate and I both laughed and told Jarvis to shut up at the same time. The bell had long ago rung, and we were still there, just listening to Jalisa vent and trying to be understanding of her pain. Once we realized the cafeteria was empty, we panicked because we were now late for the fourth period. We had no one to write us a pass to class. If you were late to class with no pass, it was automatic detention.

For the remainder of the day, all I could think about was how scared Jalisa must be to be afraid to go to bed at night in her own home. It was really bothering me that Jalisa's mom was allowing this type of stuff to go on in her home. Like, I don't really understand adults. They try to teach us right from wrong but all the while they're not being the example they need to be. She has a daughter, so she shouldn't want all those men in and out of her house like that. The things people do for money is just crazy. I say money because I know she doesn't love him or anything; she just wants the glitz and glamour he is providing her with. From the way Jalisa was explaining things, it was like the money was changing Ms. Tasha. She was letting Black and money change her relationship with her daughter, just as alcohol had done with Momma and me. All I could do was pray for Jalisa and her mom. Everything in my life was great for once. Sherry was doing so good with drinking less and less every day. I was passing all my classes, and I had the finest boy in our class.

That's right! Jarvis and I were dating. Jarvis Grant was smart, talented, sexy in every way and very respectful. Although Momma said I couldn't have a boyfriend at my age, while I was at school, I referred to Jarvis as such. J treated me like I was his whole world. He wouldn't talk to no other girl or hang out with them. I felt special, and I knew once I turned sixteen, I could really make things official with J and me. It was nice having him around, honestly. I know being around your man all the time, twenty-four-seven would drive most girls crazy, but for me, I enjoyed Jarvis' company. So far, eight grade was the best year of school I'd had. It was awesome to not have so many problems for once. It kind of made me hate that eighth grade was coming to an end. On the other hand, I was excited about the events that were coming with the end of the year. Prom was the main thing. Momma agreed that I could go with Jarvis as his date. Momma didn't know how happy I was. It was the best thing she could do for me at that moment. It wasn't even close to prom yet, and we were still happy she said yes. It was only November. The girls and I had planned to spend the whole break at my house so that Jalisa didn't have to be stuck in the house with the bad company that her mother now kept. The plan was for us to pretend to come up with the plan while at Jalisa's house after school so that Ms. Tasha wouldn't think that Jalisa had been discussing her business with us. So, we did just that. It wasn't easy trying to convince her to let Jalisa go with us, but eventually, she said yes. I was just happy for Jalisa. Finally, she could get some peace of mind. We quickly packed Jalisa's bag and were out the door! Jalisa wasn't lying when she said they were some weird people. I could see why she was afraid and staying up all night. If I were in her position, I would do the same. All that mattered was that she would be safe now for a few days. Soon as we got to my house, we raided the kitchen. We ate and ran up the stairs to my room. Jalisa and Raven went to their favorite spot, and I dived on the bed. They loved sitting in the embankment of my window seal, looking out at the night stars while we talked. The whole week we were out, all we did was eat, watch movies, and talk on the phone to Jarvis and his friends. We really enjoyed one another's company. On Thanksgiving, my mom cooked a big feast. I have to say that the break was awesome, but it was back to school time. Daily at school, Redbone, Jalisa, and I would sit and talk about prom, and it wasn't even January yet. Christmas was just around the corner. I wasn't excited about it, though. I guess you can say I was growing up. Redbone and I were sad for Jalisa, on the other hand. The things that were taking place within and around her home were taking a huge toll on her. Granted we did live in the projects, so watching people sell drugs wasn't anything new, but having those type of activities to go on within your home was different. The cops were called to her mom's house because Black beat up some crack head dude that owed him money for some product. Jalisa was scared because they had her mom, Black, and two of his workers in handcuffs. Jalisa's mom was crying and begging to be released from the cuffs, but the cops just kept yelling for her to be quiet. Jalisa just sat, wondering what would happen to her if her mom went to jail. We didn't quite understand the severity of what was going on, but we knew aggravated assault was bad. The three of us stood at the corner of the street, praying that they would take Black and release Ms. Tasha, but our prayers didn't work because the police loaded all four of them into the squad cars and drove away. Jalisa was lost. She was scared and alone. Raven and I tried to calm her down. We assured her that no matter what, we had her back. Raven packed her a bag while I sat holding Jalisa, trying to console her. We all went back to Raven's house. At first, we all just sat there in silence, unsure of what to say or think. Jalisa burst out in a rant. "I just don't understand how Momma could be so damn stupid. She is letting this ugly nigga sell drugs out our house and have all these random ass niggas running all through our shit. What the hell is she thinking about? What if child services come looking for me, what am I going to do, yawl?" "Listen, Jalisa; they aren't going to take you! We won't let them get you. You can hide out at both of our houses until your mom gets out. I'm sure she's going to call your grandparents and let them know she's locked up. We'll just let them know that you're staying with Choc and me and that our moms are OK with it so that you can go to school every day. We got you. Don't worry!" After we packed her bag, we locked up her mom's house and headed for Redbone's house just to chill after all that had just happened. No matter what we did to try and take her mind off the events of the day, Jalisa was still very upset and hurt about how things were in her life. It hurt me as a friend and as a sister to not be able to fix that aspect of her life for her. If I could just ease her pain, it would have made me feel so much better. We stayed at Raven's house that night and ate snacks and just tried to be a support system for Jalisa. That morning we got up to get dressed for school and tried to make it feel as normal as possible so that Jalisa wouldn't be upset. In school, we stayed away from the family drama because we had done enough crying and venting the previous night. During the first block, I caught wind that this boy named Kendrick was going to do a huge prom proposal for Jalisa. I was so happy because this would bring some excitement to her life in the midst of all the drama. I had no clue that Kendrick liked Jalisa, but I was happy he did. As lunchtime drew closer, I was overflowing with happiness. My girls and I never held secrets from one another, so it was killing me not to tell them what I had overheard in the hall. I didn't want to ruin it for Jalisa, so I sat at the table all antsy, waiting for the moment to come. When I saw Kendrick, all I could do was smile because I knew he had a secret crush on Jalisa. When the girls came to the table, I popped the conversation off by asking what they planned on wearing to prom and whom they were planning on going with. "As we already know, I'm going with my boo, Jarvis, of course." "Choc, it's too early to determine whom we're going with, we haven't even gone on Christmas break, and you're worried about prom," Raven said. "Just because you have a lil boyfriend, and you already know who your date is don't mean we have dates already," said Jalisa. "Well, I'm just saying if it was up to yawl, whom would you want to go to prom with?" "If it was up to me, I wouldn't go to prom with any of the boys at our school. I'll go with this boy named Anthony, who goes to East Charles Middle school with my cousin. Girl, yawl know he's super fine with pretty eyes," Raven said, smiling from ear to ear. "Where did you meet him, Redbone?" I asked out of curiosity. "Um, Choc, I saw him about three weeks ago at my cousin, Nate's birthday party. They're friends, and they play on the same basketball team. We should go to a game or something on Friday. There are a lot of cute boys that go to East Charles, girl," Redbone said. Right in the middle of Redbone lusting over this dude, she saw Kendrick walking over to our table. I started smiling and overreacting before he could even pop the question. Kendrick had a few people from the band following behind him. It was so sweet. He had Samantha Aspen to the left of him singing, "Let me love you" by Mario. In his hand, he held some beautiful flowers and a sign that read: "Beautiful Jalisa Brown, Will You Attend Prom with Me?" Jalisa was smiling and covering her face in disbelief and excitement. As Kendrick reached for her hand to pull her in to hug him, happy tears rolled down Jalisa's cheek as she laughed and laid her head on his shoulders. Raven and I were so happy that our girl was smiling and enjoying her moment in the midst of all the drama taking place in her personal life. The lunch bell rang for us to go back to class shortly after, and Kendrick and Jalisa walked to class hand in hand, smiling extra hard with excitement. Usually, people wouldn't ask people to prom until after Christmas break, so Raven wasn't bothered that Jalisa and I had dates already and she didn't. She was determined to ask Anthony to attend our prom at HighTower's Middle with her. She concocted this plan to get over to her cousin's house so that she could see Anthony. Of course, you know we were in on the plan, lol. We did everything together. Christmas break was slowly approaching, and Raven planned to spend most of the break at her aunt's house getting better acquainted with the infamous Anthony. The day before Christmas break started, Kendrick asked Jalisa to be his girlfriend. Being that both Jalisa and I had boyfriends, it made Raven more determined to get with Anthony. "Friday isn't coming fast enough," Raven said, sitting at the lunch table. Jalisa chimed in, "Why are you so ready for tomorrow? How do you know if he's even going to like you, Redbone?" "Right," I said while laughing, "he may not like light-skinned girls." "Well, tricks, we wouldn't know unless I try to holler at him, now will we?" Raven replied with an attitude. "Redbone, you know I'm just fucking with you. I hope he likes you and agrees to go to prom with you," I said. "Yawl making a bitch scared to even ask him now. I already feel desperate asking a boy to go out with me, and yawl wanna put doubt in my head," Raven said as she rolled her eyes at Jalisa and me. "Well, you know how standards go, but the way I see it, if you want it, go get it, boo. You can't wait for things to be handed to you, sometimes you have to go out on a limb. And I am Choc. I've had my bag packed from Monday!" We all burst into laughter. "Yeah, now that's desperate, Redbone," Jalisa said while still laughing. "Well, bitches, call it what you wanna. A girl gotta do what a girl gotta do." She shrugged her shoulders and left the lunch table. "Jalisa, I hope we didn't hurt Raven's feelings. You know she's a cry baby." Jalisa replied, "She shouldn't be so damn sensitive. She knows we were just playing with her. Knowing her ass, she's probably somewhere fake crying, lol." "Jalisa, yo ass doesn't have no remorse for anything," I said, chuckling a little. We left the lunchroom in search of Raven to make sure she was okay. We found her in Ms. Dixon's class writing the love note she was going to have her cousin give Anthony. "Redbone, Jalisa and I want to apologize. We didn't mean to hurt your little baby feelings. It was just a joke." Jalisa said, "Bitch, speak for yourself because I'm not apologizing. She knows it was just a joke. Redbone's ass better grow some balls." "Thanks, Choc, and fuck you, Jalisa. My feelings aren't hurt. Yawl bitches just get on my nerves always talking shit. I'm trying to write this love note that I'ma have my cousin Nate give to my soon to be new boo." We burst into laughter. "Why are you writing a note with your scary self? Just walk up to him and tell him you wanna holler at him, hell," said Jalisa. "Look, Jalisa, everyone isn't all thuggish and boyish like you. Let me do this my way." Jalisa replied, "I'm not thuggish, trick! I just like to be straightforward. But, yea, do it your way." Raven said, "And that's exactly what I plan to do." "Alright now, yawl stop with all the bickering, let's help write this letter and get my girl a boo." The three of us sat and began to put our thoughts together. I must say we formed a pretty good letter. Now, all Raven had to do was give it to him and wait for a response.

Finally, it was Friday. Raven was so excited that the weekend had come so that she could go to Nate's house. On the way to school, she went on and on about what if this and what if that. I wanted to say, "Redbone, shut the hell up already! If he's going to say yes, he'll say yeah. Damn!" "Choc, I'm just nervous. You know I don't like approaching people because I hate to be told no." Jalisa turned to Redbone and said, "Look at it this way, Redbone, if he turns your sexy ass down, then he doesn't deserve you, baby!" "You're totally right, Jalisa. I don't know why I'm tripping anyway." "It's time for first block, so I'll holler at you, bitches, later," said Chocolate. I sat in first block, just thinking and reminiscing over the years. To be so young, the girls and I had been through a lot of shit together, and now, here we are, trying to call ourselves dating and liking boys. Life's a trip, and I was kind of enjoying the ride at the current moment. Although we all were dying of anxiety, not knowing what Anthony was going to say to Raven, later, we went about our day as we normally would. Time seemed to always go by fast after lunchtime. Before we knew it, it was time to go, and operation Raven get a prom date was on the way. We didn't spend too much time talking and shooting the breeze after school like we normally would because we were on a mission, and it had to get done. As we walked to the house, we could see Jalisa's mom on their porch. We had no idea that she was going to be released from the county jail because Jalisa's grandma failed to mention that little detail to us. Simultaneously, we all stopped and just stood there with the same stupid look on our faces. We had fallen into a routine with having Jalisa at the house. "Yo, Lee-Lee, what you wanna do? Cuz we can keep walking to the house like we didn't even see her on her porch, yo." "Nah, Redbone! I'ma go holler at her, but, Choc, if it's still cool with your moms, I would like to stay with yawl for the weekend still." "Hell, yeah, Lee-Lee, you know Momma doesn't mind you being there. So, you want us to walk you over there or you good on your own?" "Thanks, Redbone, but I'm good. It's not like the broad is a killer or rapist (she chuckled a little). She just chose a stupid nigga to lay up with. I'ma just catch up to yawl in a few.... Well, Raven, I'll see you Sunday. Good luck on getting your boo." We stood, watching Jalisa walk to her front door to chat with her mom. I knew that the choices Jalisa's mom had made put a lot of stress and strain on their relationship. I just hoped that her mom would get herself together. Raven and I kept walking toward our houses. Suddenly, we heard loud talking and yelling. Jalisa and her mom were fussing. We didn't know if we should turn back around or keep walking and let them handle their personal business. We both just kind of looked at each other and kept walking. My house was before Raven's. Usually, I would continue walking with Raven, but I went into the house to inform my mom that Jalisa's mom was out of jail. I hoped that it would be an eye-opener for her, Ms. Tasha.

Chapter Eight

Prom Season

Finally, it came. Redbone, Jalisa and I had been talking about prom for months, but now it was closer to time. We had to be the baddest things in prom, so we went all out on our dresses. My mom drove us to this dress store all the way up Georgia 400.She spent about six hundred on me and Jalisa's dresses, and Redbone spent two eighty-five on hers. Our shoes came from Baker's, the hottest shoe store in Georgia at the time. Coming out of Baker's, you know we spent a nice piece of change on them. Unlike all the other girls that got their hair done by this ghetto chick named Pumpkin in the apartments, the girls and I went to the shop. Our hair and makeup were done by none other than the best. It seemed like it took all day just to get ready. I might have looked in the mirror, at least a hundred times. Jarvis, my mom, Shante, Jr and Jarvis's mom, Ms. Marissa, were rushing me to hurry and come down the stairs. "Choc, if you take any longer, we're going to miss our own prom." "OK, hold on! I'm coming down now. Yawl just have the cameras ready. Sheri, I'm serious, girl, come on! If you get any finer, I'd die of a heart attack. I'm right behind you, J baby, turn around." Everybody was in awe at how amazing I looked; all made up. My fourteen-year-old face now looked like I was every bit of twenty-one. We took lots of pictures together and with both of our families. Finally, we were in the stretch hummer with Redbone and Anthony, and Jalisa B. and Kendrick. I couldn't believe how beautiful we were. Once we got to the prom, making our grand entrance, we were all smiles. Just like we planned, we were the finest things at prom. It felt good, being in the spotlight. Jarvis and I won Prom King and Queen, while Raven and Anthony won Prom Prince and Princess. Prom was the main topic at lunch for a couple of days following prom, but it came to an end, just like all other good things. Eighth grade class trip was in another week, and that's what all the hype was about for the week. I wasn't so excited about it because the thought of graduating saddened me somewhat. I realized I would miss my teacher that played such big roles in my straight A grades and my behavior change. High school would be a whole different ball game, and I had to realize I wasn't little Chocolate, the nerd, anymore. My body was growing in ways I hadn't expected so soon. Momma said it was my hormones because I was so into Jarvis. The lusting caused the change in hormones which caused the change in my body. At the time, I didn't know what Momma meant by that, but looking back, I did now. Anyhow, I had booty, hips and a nice size chest, going into high school. I knew it would happen because I was four weeks shy of fifteen. I just didn't expect everything to sprout out at once. With the changes that took place with my body, Momma had to buy me a lot of new pants, not that I minded because I loved going shopping. I stayed in the mall, racking up on the newest shit.

It was the weekend before the class trip, so the girls and I went shopping for outfits. It was our norm to sport a new fit for every event we attended. This trip was like no other because we were also buying outfits for Raven's birthday party. She had plans for us to change outfits twice at each event. As you might know, we didn't try to outdo her on her birthday, so Jalisa and I didn't get too fancy. Once I finally made it home, I studied for my finals and helped Shante with her project for the science fair. I know it might have seemed odd that I was studying on the weekend, but that was the only way I stayed on top of my game. Saturday morning, Shante, Jr., Jarvis and I got dressed to go to the park to hang out, which was usual for us. Jarvis loved hanging with them because he knew what it meant to me. My sister and brother were my pride and joy. We were all each other had. My mom always taught us that if we had nobody else, we had each other. That Saturday morning wasn't like all the other mornings. As we were walking through the pathway to the park, Jr. stopped mid-stride and started to scream. A few steps in front of him lay a dead body. The body was of this lady named Tricia that lived in the neighborhood. It looked like she had been beaten. All her clothes were stripped off, so I assumed she probably was raped as well. Jarvis and I ran the kids back home because Jr. was very upset and scared due to the horrific scene we had just encountered. Jarvis reached for the phone to call 911 to report what we had seen. I was kind of upset that Jr. had to experience that because I tried to keep them away from that type of stuff, despite the fact that we lived in the projects.

There were police everywhere in a matter of seconds. It's crazy that her family hadn't even put a missing person's report out on her. Later that night, it was all over the news. It was the top story on all the news channels. By Sunday morning, the word in the streets was that one of the boys from the block killed Ms. Tricia. It was said that she recently started doing drugs, and she owed him some money. Everybody knew that if you got a credit, you better pay or that was your ass. They didn't give a damn who your family was or how tough they supposed to be. But who in the hell knew he would just kill her like that because she didn't have the money when she said she would? All-day in school on Monday, everywhere I turned, people were talking about what happened.

There were so many stories circling. It didn't make sense. Everybody was coming up to me, asking how the body looked when we found it and all type of stuff. Her daughters and nieces had to leave school because of all the commotion. It was a sad thing, but I was trying to focus on school because it was finals week. I was in no mood for bullshit or drama. It's a good thing I had the girls and Jarvis to keep me from going off on anybody. All that week, it was still lies and he-say-she-say. I heard this, and shawty said this going on about what happened to Ms. Tricia. Good thing was that Redbone and I passed all our tests and classes. Jalisa passed all her classes, but she had a little drama with Mrs. Tate, the English teacher. But in all honesty, Mrs. Tate just didn't like Jalisa. She said Jalisa was too fast and grown for her own good. Well, after it was all over, she changed Jalisa's grade. That still wasn't good enough, Jalisa wanted her fired or suspended for grading her unfairly. She had her momma take off work, so she could make the school take action because they weren't listening to Jalisa. Ms. Brown gave Mrs. Tate and Mrs. Russell pure hell. At the end of the meeting, the outcome was in Jalisa's favor. Mrs. Tate was suspended for the remainder of the year. It was only two weeks left for the semester, but that was enough to make Jalisa happy. After makeup testing, it was no more class for eighth grade! We were so excited to be graduating. It was like everybody was so ready for high school. The last two weeks was used for graduation practice. It was so much fun. Everybody was taking pictures and signing one another's yearbooks. You know the girls, and I had to do something different from everybody else, so we had tee shirts made for all the people we kicked it with, from time to time to sign. It was only a select few because we kept our circle small. Most of the girls weren't very fond of us, anyhow. If they knew us personally, they would know we're very nice young ladies and fun to be around. I guessed we're not their cup of tea anyway because we weren't having sex, running away from home, and everything else. Well, it's a couple of days before graduation, and we're having a PTA meeting. As it turned out, some of the parents were furious that the principal didn't want pregnant students to walk across the stage at graduation. The parents felt like it was discrimination. The board of education got involved because the parents were protesting in front of the school. As a result, the girls were made to be able to walk across the stage instead of staying seated when their names were called. Now that the madness was over, it was the big day, where girls changed from children to young women. I cried as I walked across the stage. I really don't know if I was crying because I was happy or sad. Maybe it was a mixture of both. I was kind of excited about high school but scared at the same time. High school was a whole new ball game.

Chapter Nine

⌀

New Stomping Grounds

First day of high school, oh how exciting!

"Hello?" "Hey, Ms. Lisa, it's Chocolate and Jalisa. Is Raven up for school yet?" "Yeah, baby! She is getting dressed. Hold on a second; I'll get her to the phone." "Hello?" "Hey, girl! What are you wearing?" "Man, I've changed clothes five times. What yawl wearing?" "I got on a Rocawear fit!" "And Jalisa?" "Well, Jalisa, you tell her you're on the phone." "Well, you were doing all the talking shit. Yeah, I have on a Baby Phat outfit. Put something on so we don't miss the damn bus, Redbone." "Okay, I'll meet yawl outside." "Okay, later!" We stood at the bus stop, taking pictures and talking for like five or ten minutes before the bus pulled up. School hadn't even started, and broads were already starting shit. "Jalisa, chill out! Let's just have a good day! Ignore that shit, man." "Cool, but that bitch better sit down before I throw her head through the window." "Bitch, you not gonna do shit to me!" "Whoa, whoa, whoa! Ain't gonna be no name-calling." "Jalisa, you chill, and Meeka, go sit down. Yawl just chill, shit is not that deep, man. It's the first day of school; yawl let that beef go. Choc, you need to control your girl. She is fucking reckless with her mouth." "I got her! You just go sit in your seat, and everything will be cool." "Cool! Alright, Choc." "Man, Choc, I don't know why you saved her ass because I was ready to put a bitch in her place. She thinks because she is in the tenth grade, she is all that," Jalisa said. "Don't let this freshman shit fool you. We know you'll beat her, Jalisa Brown, but like Chocolate said, chill! It's the first day of school; you don't need to get in trouble already." "Yes, Mommy dearest." "Ha, ha! Real funny trick." Finally, we made it to school, where all your classes weren't on a single hallway. I was everywhere from the basement to the third floor. I was in more advanced classes than Jalisa, but Raven and I had a few classes together. Jalisa was smart, but she played around a lot. If she applied herself, she could overachieve. Lunch was different now. In middle school, each grade level ate together, but here, everybody ate together. Only thing is, it was three different lunch hours. It was A, B and C lunches. Your lunch hour was based on your class schedule. The girls and I were lucky enough to get the same lunch period. We were in B lunch. It was hard trying to find a table because all the upperclassmen had a permanent table established already prior to us getting there. So, we grabbed a table over in the corner ducked off. "So, Red and Choc, how were your first few classes?" "Well, mine was good. There were a lot of chicks from 3rd and fourth in class with me. 3rd and fourth were a rivalry neighborhood with our hood. "Did one of them try you?" "No, Jalisa, and I'm a big girl, I can handle my own. You and Choc always treating me like a baby." "Ha, ha, ha! Redbone, I have to make sure you know how you are." "What the hell that is supposed to mean, bish? Red, you know you'll just let shit build up before you say something." "Oh, OK! I thought you were trying to call me scary." "Lol! Hell, nawl, crazy. Anyway, what about you, Choc? How were your classes?" "Well, since you asked, lol, they were good. This is going to take a lot of adjusting, but I'll manage." "Enough about us, how was yours? We see you refrained from getting into any trouble." "Funny, bitch, I'm not always in trouble. I know how to act sometimes. I can be good when I want to. Lol, but class was good. I feel like this is going to be a good year for us." "Yeah, me too! I'm glad we all here together." The lunch bell rang, and it was time for the fourth block. Fourth period was a breeze. The teacher had the class do a little ice breaker game. It was kind of fun and informative. The time went by fast. The bell was ringing, and it was time for the fifth period. You had five minutes in between each class to get to your next class—just in case you needed a restroom break or to go to your locker. We usually just used our five minutes to chat if we saw any one of us passing by. Sixth and seventh periods were a breeze as well. All the teachers pretty much had the same activities planned. The bell for dismissal rang exactly at 3:45 p.m. The next day, the girls and I decided to wear matching outfits. We each had all black BeBe jumpsuits. The one with the clear rhinestones and white Air Force Ones. The girls walked ahead of Jarvis and me as we went to the bus stop. While walking, a few boys from the Mob gang were standing at the bus stop flirting with some of the girls. I knew one of the boys because he lived next door to me. His pop's an OG in the Mob. His mom, Ms. Jean, was a hardworking woman with an awesome personality. She had two other kids besides Zo. For years, she didn't let Big Zo's drug and gang activities interfere with the life of her and the boys. I remember Zo would oftentimes spend the night at our house. He was friends with my brother DJ. He was a good kid and made pretty good grades in school. That was until Big Zo started introducing him to drugs and the gang life when he was about eleven years old. After school, he would sometimes stand on the corner with his pops. Slowly, his grades started to drop. He would miss days from school, hanging with his pops and the rest of the Mob crew. Big Zo made him think that by making his own money, he was being a man. In actuality, he was breeding him to be a product of his environment. By time Zo made it to sixth grade, he had completely dropped out of school. Ms.

Jean had no control over Zo. His dad had corrupted his mind with all types of foolishness. The streets had swallowed him. Eventually, Ms. Jean moved back to New York with her younger two boys to keep Big Zo from ruining their lives also. Zo decided to stay here in Atlanta with Big Zo. Standing on the block and in and out of juvenile. The girls teased Zo about not going to school and his clothes hanging off his behind. Zo said, "Ballers don't have to go to school because we have money to pay for everything we want." I watched as Zo, and the fair-skinned girl flirted and exchanged numbers as the bus pulled up. The freshman girl and her friends sat up front and talked about how gangster and cute Lil Zo was. As other small chatter continued on the bus, J was trying to get my attention. I was so stuck on how a mother could just give up on their child; then I realized the streets took her control over him away. It's only much you could do, and the streets had him in the chokehold. It was only one way out the Mob, and that was death. Finally, I snapped out of my daze, and Jarvis was holding a small box in his hand. The scream I let out alarmed the girls. They stood in their seat to see what was going on. Jarvis handed me a Kay's jewelry box. I opened it, and it was a diamond necklace. I hugged J so tight, smiling and tearing up at the thought. J loved me enough to buy me some jewelry. I smiled the rest of the way to school. I was shocked that he gave me a random just-because gift. I sat there, thinking to myself, "Now, I must come up on some money, so I can show him that he is appreciated." J really did whatever to make me happy. I believed he already knew what he had, and he wasn't going to let his age or the lack of gwap mess it up. He hustled every weekend, so he could spoil the both of us. Jarvis wasn't out here selling drugs and robbing people; he made his money honestly. Every Saturday and Sunday, he would walk through the nearby houses and cut grass for the people who needed his services. I liked that about him. He was different. Jarvis had dreams and aspirations just like me. We both wanted to get out the projects and live a good life. Many summer nights, we would lie in my bed with the lights out and talk about college and life outside the hood. We always talked about how we would live our life together, grow and build a family. Honestly, I couldn't wait to get out of school so that Jarvis and I could just run away and live our best lives. Only thing that would stop me was the fact that I couldn't walk away and leave my sister and brother here. Not that they would be in harm's way because Momma was doing so well now. I think we all were finally coping well with the fact that Daddy was gone and never coming back. Sometimes, I wonder if Jarvis would be the same kind of man Daddy was since they said you usually gravitate toward people like your parents. I just prayed that he's ten times better than the man my father was. Right now, he's proving that he's different than Daddy and these other niggas from the hood. That's why he's my baby and ain't nothing or nobody stopping that. "I hope these chicken heads at this high school don't think for a second that they're about to get their hands on this one because that's not going to happen. I already stamped that. He belongs to Shari "Chocolate" Parks." Ninth grade was a breeze! The girls and I made good grades, and on the weekends, our mom's let us go to the movies, parks, skating rink and stuff with the boys. We were enjoying life. We were enjoying so much that we hadn't realized that summer came so quickly. Well, Jalisa did. She was already planning to give Kendrick some nookie because she had caught him making out with this Haitian girl named Fatima. She was from Miami. Fatima had money, and she used it to sleep with whomever she wanted. She paid Ken $150 just to make out with her, but rumor had it she gave him, and two of his friends some head in the boy's locker room before school was out. Jalisa was gonna prevent that from happening again by sleeping with Ken and doing whatever else he wanted. I was against that shit, but who was I to tell her what to do with her body.

One night, we were on a 3-way call. She told Redbone and me all about her elaborate plan as to how she was gonna lose her v-card. As always, I was her alibi. So here's the plan. "I'ma tell my mom I'll be at your house for the weekend, but I don't want you to tell your mom that I'm coming. I'ma pack my clothes in my backpack. Ken's auntie gonna pick me up from the top parking lot, but we gotta walk the backstreet, so nobody will see us. We gonna spend the weekend there. Girl, I packed some lingerie. I plan to do a sexy striptease for him to show him Fatima doesn't have shit on me. I'ma tie him to a chair, so he doesn't get to touch me to make it more intense. Or should I blindfold him?" "No! Really, you shouldn't do that shit at all. Don't just fuck him cuz his cheating ass doesn't know how to keep his dick in his pants." "But who asked you, Redbone?" "Well, I'm just telling yo stupid ass. If you gonna do it, let it be for your own reasons, not just cuz this nigga wanna fuck on other girls." "I'm doing it cuz I want to. Now, mind yo damn business!" "Well, I'm about to hang up on both of y'all asses cuz all y'all do is fuss and fight." "Byc thcn, trick." "Lee-Lee, I can't stand your smart mouth ass."

Jalisa was gone the whole weekend, and her cover was not blown. I still thought she made a bad decision, but hell, it was her decision and her body. She called me early Sunday morning to say she was on the way, and I had to lie to Momma about why she was coming over so early. But once she got there, I was so ready to hear all about what had taken place. She dropped her bag, and we went right to the playground to be sure Momma wouldn't overhear our conversation. "Okay, so when I got there on Friday, we went to the park by his auntie's house just to chill. That night nothing happened. But at like 4 in the morning, I felt something warm and wet between my legs." "Bitch, what? Ken gave you some head?" "Damn, horn dog! Can I tell you the story?" (We laughed.) "Okay, hurry up to the juicy part." "So he was licking and sucking my thighs, and each time he went from one leg to the next, he would lick my pussy just a little. I was moaning and begging him to fuck my pussy with his tongue. He told me to relax and let my juices flow. He started fingering me and sucking my clitoris at the same time. I could feel my pussy getting so wet, and the sound of him slurping up all my sweet goodness was driving me wild. I kept saying, 'Fuck me, Daddy. Fuck me!' but he was like, 'We'll save that for later.' He ate me for like an hour. I had orgasms after orgasms! Finally, he stopped. I wanted to give him some head, but I was drained. We went back to sleep. A few hours later, I woke up to the smell of bacon, cooking in the kitchen. So, I went to wash my face and brush my teeth, and Kendrick was sitting on the bed with a plate of food and orange juice. He was showing out, so I knew I had to bring my A-game when it was my turn. For the rest of the day, we just chilled and watched TV. We played cards, and he cooked us some dinner. Soon as night time hit, I couldn't wait to pop this pussy for a real nigga, lol. So, we took a shower together! In the shower, he was kissing me so passionately and looking in my eyes. If this wasn't love, man, I don't know what to call it. But anyway he washed my body, and then we got out. I told him to meet me in the living room. I put the lingerie on, turned some slow jams on through the sound system and walked out the bathroom into the living room. His mouth dropped. As he reached out to grab me, I shook my head, 'No, no!' and popped the tie that I was about to use to tie his hands. He smiled and leaned back in the chair. I slowly walked over to him, smiling and licking my lips. Once I had his hands tied, I kissed his lips and down to his stomach. I could see his dick getting hard, so I bagged up. I bent over in front of him while doing a slow whine. I was spinning and touching him. I made him tell me how much he wanted it. I gave him a lap dance. The whole time, he was busy trying to position himself to stick his hard erect penis in me, but I wouldn't let him. It wasn't time yet. I had to show him the tricks I learned from watching Black and Tasha flicks. He begged for me to let him feel my insides. So, I got on my knees in front of him and started kissing the head. He was moaning so loud. I could feel my own juices running down my legs. I slowly swallowed his whole penis down to the shaft. I was sucking and squeezing his balls, and just when he was about to ejaculate, I took it out my mouth and let him cum all on my face." "Bitch, you a freak! You sure this was your first time doing this shit?" "Yea, I'm sure, Choc, but I been watching Momma and Black pornos. Let me finish telling y'all dang. So, I untied him, and he laid me down on the floor. He kissed me from my head to my feet. Girl, the boy sucked my toes! Oh, it made me horny, and my pie tingled. OK, so he was sucking my toes and fingering me at the same time. Then he kissed his way back up to the middle. Spread my legs wide and ate me like it was his last meal before electrocution. Right when he was about to stick it in, I stopped him. 'Ken, you know I'm a virgin, right?' 'Yea, I know. I promise to take my time with you, baby. I wanna enjoy all of this.' So, I took a deep breath, and he slid it in slowly. He was kissing me and talking to me to take my mind off the fact that he was trying to open me up. Finally, when he had all of his big cock in me, he looked into my eyes while biting his bottom lip, sliding in and out. With each stroke, he dug deeper. A single tear rolled out the corner of my eye, and he kissed it away. He stopped and ate my pussy again, and by this time, I was about to explode! Y'all, that was the best feeling I ever felt. Before I had the chance to cum in his mouth, he stuck it back in, and we both climaxed at the same time. He held me until I fell asleep." "Bitch, all that shit y'all did, you can't tell me you were a virgin. You've been holding a secret, Lee-Lee!" "Choc, I swear I wouldn't lie to y'all. This was the first time." "Redbone, what you think? This bitch lying, ain't she? Lol!" "Yea, she had had that lil thang played with before." "Lol, man, believe what y'all want. But I know this won't be the last time. While not the last time, I gave him some head cuz even though he took his time, the sex hurt a lil bit. The way my mouth watered when I was sucking him, I liked it and the sound of him moaning, pulling my hair and calling my name." For the rest of the summer, Jalisa had me thinking about losing my virginity. I wanted it to be special, just like that.

Chapter Ten

Sweet Sixteen

Where do I begin? Here I was in tenth grade and contemplating sexual acts when, in reality, I needed to be thinking about which college I would attend. I knew whatever school I was going to had to be the same school Jarvis would attend. He was on our school's junior varsity basketball squad and had multiple college scouts looking into recruiting him. I didn't wanna seem like my whole life revolved around him, but I wanted to spend my whole life with him. Don't get me wrong, J didn't wanna be without me either. We were friends before anything. We made a promise to always have each other back, no matter what, and that was a promise I planned to keep. School was off to a great start with no drama. Man, I was enjoying life. It was a week to Labor Day holiday, and I was sure Jarvis and I would be laid up somewhere. I had him to ask his big brother if we could chill at his spot since he and his baby momma had just got a new place. I was so happy when he told me his brother said it was cool. That weekend, I had my momma's car. So, the girls and I went to the mall. Lee-Lee helped me pick out some sexy ass lingerie, and I was hot and ready. Seemed like the week wasn't going fast enough, and Jarvis kept trying to talk me out of it. He kept saying, "Baby, we have our whole lives ahead of us. It's no rush! When the time's right, we'll get our time." Nigga the time was right, and the time was now! It kind of made me feel like he wasn't attracted to me. I didn't tell J how I felt because I knew the type of personality he had, and it wasn't that. But I couldn't help how his actions made me feel despite that. So, finally, it was Labor Day weekend. I told my mom that I would be at Raven's cousin's house with her because that was the plan. Jarvis and I caught the transit to his big brother's house. I was so excited that it was finally about to happen. After two buses and a train, we finally made it. He introduced me to his brother's baby momma, and we went into the spare room to drop our bags. I asked if it was okay if I took a shower because I was so hot and sweaty. His brother handed me a washcloth and towel and directed me to the restroom. While I was showering, I was preparing my mind for what I was about to do. In all honesty, I wasn't ready, but I was if that made sense. At first, I could hear them laughing and talking, then suddenly it was quite. I hurried to get out the shower to see what was going on. I had eighteen missed calls from Raven. My mom had shown up at her house to get me. I had no idea why she would just pop up. I was scared out my mind and didn't know what to do. I couldn't tell her where I was. It would take me all night to get there by transit. I paced the floor for at least 5 minutes, trying to think of a good lie before I called my momma to explain why I wasn't where I was supposed to be. Finally, I thought about Jarvis' brother's new baby and just said that we had to go to the hospital because something was wrong with his niece. I called my momma. I was shaking and breathing hard as if she was standing right in front of me. "Hello, Momma?" "Shari, where the hell yo grown sneaky ass at? I been to Lisa's house and yo grown-ass wasn't there, so you better have a good fucking reason why you weren't there when I came!" "Momma, if you let me explain, I can tell you! Jarvis' brother's baby had to be rushed to the hospital, and the baby was only a few days old. He was scared and crying and asked me to go with him. When I left, Ms. Lisa wasn't home, yet that's why she didn't know I was there." "You a damn liar. You haven't been there because the lady next door said the only people she had seen go in and out were Redbone and Lee-Lee. So, tell another fucking lie." "Momma, I swear that lady is lying on us. I was there today. J and I just left there about two hours ago. And we were waiting for his brother to bring me home. They were trying to make sure the baby was stable first." Whole time in my head, I was asking God to forgive me for speaking such evil over that sweet innocent baby. I had gone through all this trouble and didn't even get my stuff played with. I was quiet and pissed off the whole way home. I'm not sure if I was madder that I didn't get none or because Ms. Ellis' fat nosey ass caused me to get grounded! I hated being stuck in the house, and I knew she was gonna take my phone, and I wouldn't be able to talk to J. Times like this, I missed Daddy because I knew he would just give me a talk about the birds and the bees and just let me off the hook. But Momma was so extra! I kissed J goodnight before we even reached the parking lot because I knew if she saw that, it would just piss her off more. His brother backed me up on my story, but Momma still wasn't going for that shit. I was grounded for three weeks. No outside, no phone, and no girls.

My punishment was finally over, and I was so excited that I could finally see the girls. Momma wasn't sure if she wanted me to date Jarvis still but little did she know I was the one trying to persuade him to have sex with me. Now that my plan had failed, I had to come up with a new plan and to plan strategically. Jarvis wasn't able to come inside Momma's house no more, but I knew it wouldn't be long before she would be out late with Ms. San's drunk ass, and I was gonna make my move then. I hoped it would be around my birthday or Jarvis's because that would be perfect timing. I had two weeks to my birthday, and I was excited! I didn't really want a big party or nothing; I just wanted to go out to eat or something with Jarvis and the girls. I begged Momma for a week straight to let us use her car to go eat and to the teen club on the Southside. All she kept saying was she would think about it, so I told J to hit us his brother cuz he never told us no. And just like I expected, he told J he could get one of his cars as long as we had the gas fare. That was a no brainer. I just knew that was our way to take our relationship to the next level. I tried all week to stay on Momma's good side so she wouldn't ruin my birthday plans. Friday had come so fast, and I didn't have an outfit for the club, and Momma said she wasn't supplying me money to eat, club and look fashionable because my birthday was only one day, and she had bills. So, the girls and I went to the mall. Let's just say I jumped fly at someone else's expense. Saturday morning, I went to Punkin to get the infamous snatch back ponytail, to the nail shop and to get my brows waxed. I was ready to party. I planned for J and me to hit his brother's crib, so we were leaving the club an hour earlier so I could make it home before my curfew. The birthday dinner was a success. I got plenty of gifts, but none beat the gift Lee-Lee's ole freaky ass gave me. It was a "pop that cherry bag" as she called it. It was filled with condoms, body oils, some handcuffs and chocolate syrup. I didn't know what the hell to do with all that stuff, but I planned to figure it out. When I got to the club, I wasn't even feeling the vibe. I just wanted to go rock J's world! An hour into the party, J and I snuck out. The girls had a ride home, so I wasn't worried about that. I was all over J before we could even get in the house. Kissing and trying to rip his clothes off. He was just so damn sexy and smelled so good. Once in the house, Jarvis picked me up and carried me to the spare room. He laid me on the bed and slowly undressed me. In my head, I couldn't believe it was finally about to happen. He kissed me so passionately my whole body shivered. I rolled on top of

Jarvis, looking in his eyes, trying to see through his soul. I kissed him, sucking his bottom lip as I pulled away. I pulled his shirt over his head while I was rolling my hips on top of him. I could feel his penis getting hard up under me. I kissed his neck and down to his chest. I traced his chest with my tongue and down to his stomach. I unbuttoned his pants and pulled them off. Jarvis was about to sit up. I pushed him down and slowly caressed his shaft in my hand. Unsure of what to do, I kissed the tip of his penis all the way down to his balls. As I worked my way back up, kissing and sucking the sides, I put it in my mouth. I could hear him gasp for air. I sucked him and licked him in places he probably never imagined. Just as he was about to cum, he pushed me away and laid me down on my stomach. He lifted my hips slightly in the air. He put his head in my butt and eat my soul out. He was licking my ass and fingering my pussy, and I was moaning and rubbing my nipple. He flipped me over and began eating my pussy and fucking me with his tongue. I was moaning and grinding against his tongue. I was about to climax, but I was slightly startled when he stuck his middle finger in my ass. I was so ready to feel Jarvis' penis inside of me. I started closing my legs, trying to push him from between my legs. I kept moaning, "Okay, baby! Okay!" J realized I had had enough, and he kissed his way up. Placing kisses all up and down my thighs and stomach up to my neck and lips. Finally, I could feel his penis in the opening of my vagina. I opened my legs slightly and arched my back. J whispered in my ear, "I love you," just as he slid his dick in me. I gripped the sheets tightly in my hands and buried my head in the covers. He stroked in and out a few times before he rolled me over onto my back. Before he inserted himself back in me, he just lay on me, kissing me. He went down and ate me some more and flipped me over again. He went down to my breast and began sucking it. I put his hand between my legs so he could play with my pussy while he sucked my titties. He came up, and in one motion, he was slowly stroking me. We were kissing and sweating. After a few minutes, we both climaxed. J collapsed on top of me, and we both just lay there. I wanted to just indulge at the moment, but I knew I had to make it home before my curfew. I kissed Jarvis and told him we had to get up. I ran to the restroom to wash up when I noticed cum running down my legs.

I stood in the mirror in shock for a few minutes. How the hell we forgot to use a condom. Tears started to well up in my eyes, and at that moment, I was scared. Jarvis came in and hugged me from behind and kissed the back of my neck before he realized I had tears in my eyes. He spun me around, grabbing my face. "What's wrong, my love? Did I do some wrong?" "No, not really, but I just realized we didn't put a condom on, J! What if I end up pregnant? What we gonna do then?" "Baby, baby, listen. I love you, and whatever happens, we'll deal with it together." "Okay, but, J, I'm not ready for no baby. I have my whole life ahead of me." "We both do, Choc, but whatever happens, we'll deal with it. Get dressed so you can make it home in time or Ms. Sherry gonna kill us both, and we won't have to worry about no baby." We laughed, and he kissed me and walked out the bathroom. We rode in the car in complete silence. No music, no talking. Completely quiet, drowning in our thoughts. Once I got home, I showered and cried and prayed while I was in there. I lay in the bed like, "How could I be so stupid to forget to tell him to put the condom on? I was just so ready to get my rocks off I wasn't even thinking or using my head. Momma gonna kill me if I end up pregnant. It was bad enough she had to raise us on her own. ." I could barely sleep. I lay in the bed, tossing and turning and praying to God in between. I don't think I'd ever prayed this hard about anything in my life. I just refused to be a teenage mother still in high school with a baby. I barely came out the room on Sunday. I told the girls I had a lot of homework to catch up on, so I didn't have to be bothered with them asking about how my sex escapade went. I couldn't tell them we didn't use a condom, and now my stupid ass could end up pregnant. I didn't take many of Jarvis' calls maybe because I was just so mad and irritated by the whole situation. Now don't get me wrong, he fucked me so good. I wanted some more and some more but not at this expense.

A month had passed. I was too scared to have sex again, but I would give J head a few time a week just to keep him satisfied. He kept trying to tell me the damage was already done so we might as well keep doing it, but I was like, "What if it isn't?" Hell, I wasn't about to help increase the chances by continuing to let him fuck me raw. He wanna scream he could pull out, but he should've done that the first time around. My period was due to come three days past, and there was still no sign of it. I knew I couldn't tell Momma or that would be the end of Jarvis and me. I wasn't ready to lose the man of my dreams, so I came to the conclusion that I had to break my silence and tell the girls about what was going on. It was killing me anyway to keep a secret from them, but I just didn't want them to judge me. Especially Jalisa's black ass. I called Raven first to see if she could ask her cousin, Kim, to take me to the abortion clinic. "Raven?" "What's up, Chocolate? You must be in some serious shit cuz that's the only time you call me Raven. What's up, bitch? What's going on?" "Man, Momma gonna kill me, Red." "What? Why?" "Okay, so you know J and I left the club early and went to his brother's house to have sex. The shit was so good I didn't even think to ask this nigga if he had a condom on. So we were just fucking, switching positions and all kind of shit. This fool nutted in me two times! And my fucking period hasn't come. I need you to see if Kim will take me to get an abortion. She can't tell nobody, and you can't either. Not even Lee-Lee!" "Damn, Choc! Okay, okay, I'ma call her to see, but you know Jalisa gonna be mad if we keep this from her." "I know, Redbone, but you gotta promise me this one we gonna take to the grave, just you and I. I can't even tell Jarvis that the test came back positive, and I'm getting an abortion. He would want me to keep the baby, but I can't be no teen mom, Redbone. I wanna go to college and get the fuck out the hood, man. I can't be in college with no baby on my hip, you know." "I understand where you're coming from. Hell, we all wanna get the hell away from here. I promise to sweep this shit under the rug." "Cool, hit me back after you talk to Kim, please." "I got you." I hung up the phone and started to think how I was gonna hide this shit from my momma. Just as I was good into my nap, Raven called me back and said Kim could take me on Thursday. I was excited, but I had to figure out how I would get four hundred dollars to pay for the shit. Soon as we hung up, I called Keem cuz I knew he always had my back. Quan was locked up so I couldn't call him, but I wished that he was home cuz he gave me whatever, no questions asked. I dialed up Keem. "Keem, I need a favor, cousin, a big favor." "What's up, Chocolate? You know I got you on whatever, whenever." "I really need four hundred dollars. I'll give it back, or I can run-up in the mall and get some shit for you and your girl to pay it off." "Hell, naw! I've told yo ass about stealing out the mall, man. You better get you one of these trap niggas and play them out their money. You pretty as hell. I know they be at yo neck. They ain't gonna try you cuz you my lil cousin, and they already know how Quan, Tj and I come about you. So they gonna cut a check with you. You just gotta spit game to these lames. We taught you enough to be a Queen Pin out here." "Man, yo ass crazy. They all scared to talk to me cuz they knew you gonna kill some." "Hell, yea if they don't treat you right, but I got you. Walk down to the spot later on."

"Okay, I love you, cousin. Be safe!" "You already know. Aye! If auntie cooked, bring me a plate." "Okay, I got you. See you later." I lay in bed with a million thoughts in my head, and one for sure was that I was going to hell for what I was about to do. "How do you kill something God created?" To make it all make sense, I asked myself why God would give me a baby to raise in these bullshit conditions. So I thought I was making the best decision not to keep the baby because I couldn't provide it with the life it deserved. It started getting dark, so I got out of bed, washed my face and gave myself a prep talk in the mirror. Like, "It's no use in feeling sorry and down on myself now. I should've been more responsible. Now I had to do what I had to do." As I was walking to Keem's spot, I noticed this dude that I had a huge crush on when I was younger. He used to be a bomb, but now the nigga was getting bread. The closer I got to him, the more I put a lil extra twist to my walk. I noticed them breaking their necks. I smiled and kept walking. But I heard them whispering, and I was sure that everything Keem had just said earlier that day was true.

"Here I am, sitting in a damn abortion clinic, looking crazy, scared, and confused. I never thought I would be one of the girls I talked about for sitting up in here, killing God's creation. But I also never thought I would be so damn foolish to be letting some nigga hit me raw. I was more responsible, or at least, that's what I thought, but now I see how it is so easy to be caught up in the moment. Jarvis was kissing and licking me in places I had never explored, and I didn't have a care in the world. Now here I am making a decision I will later regret." Lost in my thoughts, I didn't hear the nurse calling my name. Kim tapped my shoulder and scared the shit out of me. It was as if I had forgotten where I was. I was in another space, imagining how my life would be if I wasn't here and if I had told Jarvis about me being pregnant. I was watching us lying on the floor, playing with this brown-skinned curly headed baby in an apartment I had never been in. The little girl had the perfect laughter I had ever heard. She was perfect in every way. For a moment, I wanted to change my mind and walk right out that damn place, but I knew I had to do this for the betterment of my future. I stood up, and my knees felt weak. Instantly, I thought maybe this was a sign from God that I wasn't supposed to take my ass back there and lie on them folk's table. But somehow my feet moved themselves and walked me right on to the back. I was out of my mind. A few hours later, I awoke to some strange looking old lady asking me how I felt and the name of the person who brought me in so they could bring the car around. She stepped out, and another heavyset younger lady came in to help me get my clothes on. I lay back on the cold bed with tears in my eyes, feeling horrible about what I had done, but it was too late for all that now. I barely heard the instructions on how to take medicine. I was just ready to get home and lie down. I knew I needed to get myself together in time before Momma came home. Redbone pretended to be sick so she could stay home and soon as I hit my front door, she came, knocking. She just lay in the bed with me, rubbing my back without saying a word. We ended up falling asleep then suddenly we heard a loud bang downstairs. I was too drained from the medicine to get up just yet, but Redbone went downstairs to see. No one was in the house, but she could hear the commotion outside. She yelled upstairs to me that someone was outside fighting. Too scared to open the door she ran upstairs, and we watched from the window. I fell back against the wall and took a deep breath. "Redbone, I feel horrible for killing my baby, but seeing shit like this was the reason I had to do it. I can't raise no baby in this type of fucked up environment. Motherfuckers killing people they grew up with and selling crack rocks to their own partners mommas. This shit ain't no life for a child." "I know,

Choc, and I respect your decision. You did what was best for you." "I know, but if J finds out, he gonna hate me for this shit. All he kept talking about was if I was pregnant, then we could get our own spot and work when we got out of school. But how the fuck were we supposed to have a decent life working at Mickey D's or some shit, paying rent and taking care of a child? Shid, I guess, struggle like our parents." "I don't know really, Shari, but you made the right choice. Stop crying and get some rest like you said, we taking this shit to the grave. Jarvis will never know." "I love you, Raven." "I love you too, baby! Get some rest before your mom comes back."

After that day, Redbone and I never spoke of the situation again. But shit was starting to change with J and me. I never would have thought that we would be in this place. I guessed he didn't really love me like he said he did. He was just like all the other boys, as it turned out. He claimed we were too young to be trying to settle down and that we should explore our options for a while or stay together and have an open relationship. Whatever the fuck that meant, but I wasn't about to share no man with another bitch. I wasted my V-card on this nigga, and I hated myself for it. Kinda made me feel like I should've just fucked Marcus. I couldn't take him talking to other girls and sitting in the cafe with different bitches. So, eventually, I broke things off with Jarvis, and I couldn't help but think I made the right decision not to keep that baby. I noticed the change in his behavior a few months after we had sex: he started dressing differently, talking and walking differently. He thought he was the man, and these nappy head hoes were boosting his ego. Little did he know I was being respectful of our relationship and turning niggas down for him. Now that I had this banging body, all the d-boys from the hood were at my neck. Niggas that were getting paper. And I was trying to be faithful to this nigga. But now, I was about to turn my savage up on his ass. I planned to make him regret he let me get away.

Chapter Eleven

Beast Mode

Tenth grade was a year of blessing and lessons, but I was on an entirely different level now. I had discovered the world of sex and profits and how to use what I had to get what I wanted. Now don't get me wrong, I wasn't just out there fucking everything that moved, but that's what everyone thought—that's how it all started. After I was done crying over Jarvis' ass, I started kicking it at my cousins' spot. I met this nigga named Plug. Everybody called him Plug cuz he was the weight man. He invited me to his mansion party that he had every year. I was too young to attend, but since he personally invited me, I was able to attend. I told him if I was coming, I had to bring my girls with me, and he said it was cool. We just couldn't come in no childish swimsuits. I laughed and told him not to worry. Soon as he left, I ran to the restroom to call the girls. I told them to meet me at the playground cuz I didn't want Keem to hear me bragging about Plug. Plug was one of his few friends that he said was off-limits. Truth be told, he only made me want him more. I knew Plug was a boss and what better way to piss J off than to mess with a nigga that could give me more than he ever did. I told Keem I would come back later that I was going to chill with the girls. Since we were growing up, Keem always had a crush on Lee-Lee, but that's just cuz he heard about all the freaky shit she did with her man. As I was walking out, he said, "Tell Jalisa, when she is ready to get spoiled and have all the hoes mad at her, to come holla at me." I laughed and said, "Okay!" I ran to the park so anxious to tell the girls about Plug inviting me to the mansion party. Out of breath as I reached my porch, I realized the girls weren't there yet. "Raven, where the hell y'all at?" "Here, we come! Lee-Lee had to do something for Ma Tasha." "Oh, OK, girl. My fat ass is tired. I ran up here, thinking y'all were gonna beat me here. But it's okay. I'm here, see you in a sec." I went to my back door to get something to drink. I grabbed the soda off the door of the refrigerator, and I couldn't help but overhear Momma talking on the phone. It sounded like she was talking to a man. But I had no time to be nosey; I had to let the girls know the move for the weekend. I sat on the porch waiting for them to show up. I was so excited cuz I knew Plug was the man, and he cashed all his girls out. "Finally y'all bitches show up!" "Man, bitch, I had to do something for my momma. What's so damn urgent that you needed us here ASAP?" "Okay, so y'all know Plug, right?" "Yea!" "Yea! So he invited me to his mansion party. I told him I couldn't come without y'all, and he was cool with that. He said we couldn't come in there looking childish cuz we gonna be the only young girls. It's a grown folk's party." "Hell yea, Choc, I'm down!" "I knew you would be, Lee-Lee, but what about you, Redbone?" "Man, I don't know about that cuz you know how y'all bitches get when y'all drink. And I'm not babysitting nobody's pussy but my own." "Man, bitch, it was just once that Jalisa got drunk, so don't worry about that. I'm trying to snatch me a baller, so I don't have to run up out the mall no more. A lil fucking ain't never hurt nobody, lol." "Well, Raven, I promise to behave if you go with us! It's no fun if the whole gang is not involved." "Okay, okay! Don't try to use the sad puppy dog eyes on me. I'll go, but I'm not with no bullshit y'all." "Okay, Redbone! No bullshit, we promise." The next day, the girls and I went shopping for swimsuits. I paid for everybody's stuff with the money Plug gave me. We were so excited about going; I didn't even think how Keem was gonna feel with me being there or the fact that Plug invited me. But I was a big girl, and I could hold my own.

It was the day of the party, and Plug hadn't even called me since he gave me the money to get something to wear. I was a bit wary about that, but hell, even if he didn't call, I was still showing up to that party. With all this ass and hips, somebody had to witness this greatness. I even put some makeup on to make myself appear a lil bit older. I walked to Jalisa's house to get her and then to Redbone's house. I had on sweats over my swimsuit so Momma wouldn't see it cuz nothing was stopping me from hitting the party. It was one of the biggest pool parties ever, and I was finally able to attend. We hopped on the bus and all Lee-Lee, and I could think of was how we were about to run up a check. Redbone's ole lovable ass wasn't with that, but hell, it beat stealing out the mall any day. I really just wanted to make Jarvis regret that he fucked me over. We hopped off the bus a block from where the party was so that no one would see us get off the bus. When we got to the gate, the guard asked us our names and permitted us to come in. Plug had us listed as Chocolate and friends. I felt like the HBIC. We headed over for one of the empty cabanas and ordered a drink. In my head, I wanted to find Plug and figure out why he hadn't hit me up, but I knew I needed to play it cool. I didn't wanna come off as a bugaboo. After a few minutes of chatting with the girls, I noticed Plug talking to this dude over by the DJ's booth. I nodded my head, "What's up?" And he nodded back. It was kinda irritating me that he wasn't all up in my face, but I was sure he probably had some other hoes he fucked with there. The crowd started to get thick. The girls and I moved closer to the pool so we could be seen. Jalisa and I had on a monokini low cut in the back; Redbone had on a thong two-piece. Keem was mad that I had my whole ass out, but he said if I was gonna be acting grown, I better be prepared to deal with what came along with being grown. Little did he know I was already mentally prepared for it for months now.

A group of guys walked over to the edge of the pool where we were sitting and started making small talk with us. Lee-Lee excused herself to go get us another drink. I was actually feeling the vibe from the guys. We were all laughing and enjoying the moment. Just as Lee-Lee walked back up, our song came over the speakers. We all yelled, "That's my jam." Any time Juvenile song back that ass up came up, you could guarantee all the females would drop it like it's hot. We were bent over shaking with our drinks still in our hands. Spilling liquor, having a good ole time when I felt a tight grip on my arm pulling me. "What the hell, Plug?" "Bitch, you think I invited you here to be shaking yo ass on these broke ass punks? Bitch?" "Hold up! I ain't nobody's bitch! Not yet!" "You ain't, but you still not gonna disrespect me in my shit!" "Hell, it's not like you've been paying my ass any attention! I been here for hours and all you've done was nod yo damn head at me. I'm just trying to have a good time!" "Well, have a good time some other way besides disrespecting me, shaking yo ass on these other niggas." As he walked off, he pushed me into the pool. I was so embarrassed and pissed off that he fucked my hair up. I didn't plan on getting wet! I just wanted to sit by the poolside, looking cute. Since I was already wet, I grabbed a float and hopped on it. The girls kept talking to the guys while I floated around the pool for like five minutes. I knew Jalisa was gonna have some smart shit to say, so I just prepared myself for the bullshit. Redbone walked away from the guys and joined me in the water. "Hey, Chocolate, you good girl?" "Yea, Redbone, I'm good. That nigga just tripping. He is mad cuz niggas are showing me attention, but hell, it's not like he was trying to. I know Keem gonna go off on me later, but I'm a big girl. I can handle his ass. That shit is actually a turn on. I got the biggest dope boy in his feelings about my lil young ass." "Girl, yo ass crazy. Here comes Jalisa's big mouth ass." "I know she is gonna have some smart shit to say." "Hell yea! It's not right if she doesn't." "Choc, what the fuck was that?" "Man, I don't damn know. He was mad that I was dancing with a dude. Said I was madly disrespectful." "But why the fuck did he push you into the water?" "It's a pool party, ain't it, Lee-Lee?" "I'm just saying that shit looked mad and aggressive." "Well, it wasn't, so don't think too much about it." I grabbed Redbone a float and told her to get on it, trying to dismiss the conversation. I noticed other girls started getting in the water and guys started diving in with girls in their arms. The party was jamming. I was trying to enjoy myself, but in my head, I was thinking that the nigga was crazy, although I liked all the shit. As it started getting dark, I was about ready to go. I wasn't drinking nothing else Coz Keem was drunk, and I had to drive his car back to the hood for him. He was riding with this Hoe Erica whom he is messing with. She didn't really like me cuz she felt like I wanted my cousin all to myself, but that was some sick shit. I was about to get out the water when Plug and his right-hand man came walking over to the edge of the pool where we were. "Yo, Choc, let me rap with you for a sec." I gave him the side-eye and hopped up on the edge of the pool. "Nawl yo, I wanna talk to you in private." "How is it private when yo shadow is with you?" "He is good; I just don't want yo nosey ass friends in our business. I see how yo girl keeps looking at me." "Boy, fuck you! I'm not looking at you. I'm just trying to make sure my sister is straight," Lee-Lee shouted at Plug. "Chill, Lee-Lee! I'm OK. I got this." "Okay! It's cool, Choc, long as you good." I walked to the side of the cabana with Plug. The whole time, I could see the girls staring us down. Jalisa really didn't like that Plug pulled my arm like that or that he pushed me into the pool. But I was good; it wasn't like he hurt me. "What's up, man?" "Listen, Choc; I'm sorry about that cuz I don't even put my hands on women, yo. But that shit had me hot yo. You over there shaking yo ass on them lames, and I haven't even felt that juicy thang bounce on me yet. I invited you here for me." "Okay, but you didn't say not one word to me before you came over there on that bullshit, Plug." "Yo! I said I apologize. How about I take you shopping to make it up to you? And you can bring yo lil homegirls too so the smart mouth bitch can shut up." "Listen, don't be calling her out her name, that's my sister. And don't be putting your hands on me." "Okay, Ma! I'll see you in the morning with yo lil fine ass." Plug walked off, and I couldn't help but smile. I jumped back in the pool. "So, y'all bitches ready to go shopping tomorrow?" I screamed excitedly. "Hold on! Shopping? This nigga taking you shopping cuz he pushed you into the water?" "Yep! He said it's his apology, and he even said you and Ms. Big Mouth could come too." "Yes, bitch, I need some new shit anyway! Thanks, Choc's new boo." "Damn, Lee-Lee! Since when you don't get excited about getting some shit that we don't have to steal?" "Man, I can tell I'm not gonna like that nigga, but I'm not turning down no free shit. So what time I need to be ready?" "Lol, man, I don't know! But listen, you act like the nigga blacked my eye or some shit. He just pushed me into the water. I can handle me, and you already know I'm not about to tolerate no nigga putting his hands on me. So don't worry about that. Plus he's not for you to like; you not the one fucking him." "Wait! So y'all fucked, and you didn't tell us?" "No, Redbone, I haven't, at least not yet. Now get y'all shit and let's go." Soon as we were walking out the gate, Plug's shadow walked up on us. "Excuse me, beautiful in the two-piece." "Yes?" "You mind if I chop it up with you for a sec." "Yeah, I do really. Sorry, I'm not interested, I have

a boyfriend." "Keyword, Boy. He can't do for you what I can."
"You right! He probably doesn't have as much money as you do,
but he loves me, and I know I don't have to play second to no one
with him." "Yeah, alright! Be like that then with yo stuck up ass,
but I'll catch you on the rebound." We kept walking. "Damn,
Redbone, you didn't have to be so cutthroat." "Unlike y'all, I love
my boyfriend, and I'm not trying to put up with no bullshit just for
some money." "Well, hell, Choc and I are trying to scheme our
way out this shit. Don't get me wrong, I love Kendrick but his lil
McDonalds check working a few hours a day after school isn't
gonna get us out of that hell hole we live in." "That's why y'all
bitches need to stay in school, go to college and get y'all damn
selves out the hood." "Lol! Yeah, Ok, all that shit sounds good,
and I do plan to graduate and go to college, Redbone, but I'ma still
run me up a check on these niggas if they willing to spend it."
"Yeah, for real, Redbone." "Choc, you right about this free money
man. Y'all bitches let money run y'all, but that shit ain't free, you
paying for it. Every time, that nigga snatches yo ass up for doing
some he doesn't like." "Nawl! That shit dead! He is not doing that
no more after our talk." "Yeah, okay, Choc! We'll see."

The next morning, I woke up super early. I fixed the kids some
breakfast and cleaned the kitchen back up cuz I knew Momma
would be coming to start her Sunday dinner soon. I heard the
phone ring as I was running up the stairs. I dived on the bed and
answered it in a hurry. Just as I expected, it was Plug on the other
end. "Hello?" "What's up, Choc?" "Hey! What's up, Plug? You
ready?" "I'm about to head over for yo cousin's spot to drop
something off. Can you meet me there?" "I'm not even dressed. I
just got out the bed really." "Okay, well, get yo ass dressed and
meet me there." "Yeah, alright." I hung up and ransacked my
closet, looking for something cute to put on. I jetted out the house,

not realizing I forgot to call the girls. I was halfway to Keem's spot when I realized it and had to turn around. "I don't know why I am rushing, his ass can wait." Soon as I reached Raven's house, her momma was on the porch, talking to Ms. Ellis' nosey ass. "Hey, Ms. Lisa, is Redbone woke?" "Yeah, baby! She's up in there, cleaning up. What? Y'all getting into this early?" "Oh, nothing! We just going to hang out downtown." "Y'all asses better not be down there stealing cuz I'm not bailing her ass out no more." "No, ma'am, we're not." I ran into the house. "Redbone, let's go, Plug is waiting for me!" "Damn! Why you yelling? His ass can wait." "Man, tell Ken you gotta go cuz I need to call Jalisa so she can meet us at Keem's spot." "Baby, I'ma call you back. This rude bitch wanna use the phone." I called Lee-Lee, and she was already up and ready, despite all the shit she was talking about not liking Plug. On the walk, we talked about all the stores we were going to hit. Redbone ole sensitive ass was the only one worried about how many other bitches he had made this offer to. I could fucking care less because it was my turn now; the rest of them bitches is history!

Chapter Twelve

Free Bands

I see why these females wanna be ballers' wives so damn bad. Running in and out of stores in the mall, not having to look at the price tags and still get everything you want. This shit was an adrenaline rush. I could get used to this. "Say, Choc, you got enough bags yet?" "Not really! Babe, I haven't gone in all the stores I like yet. Well, I hate to spoil your fun, but I gotta go make a play. Don't hit me with the sad eyes. Here go ten bands, you and your girls enjoy the rest of y'all day. I'll catch you later. I got another surprise for you." "What? You have more planned? Babe, this is more than enough." "Nawl, they say make the first impression the best, right?" I don't think I'd ever smiled so hard. "Thanks, babe." I turned back to the girls and did a silent scream! "Bitch, he just gave me ten bands for us to continue shopping, but he gotta go make a play." "Wait! How the fuck are we getting home?" Lee-Lee asked. "Damn, Lee-Lee, you just don't let up, do you? You think he's going to leave me, us stranded? Fuck! You'll mess up a wet dream. He's sending an errand boy to pick us up when we're done. I'ma drop y'all off and go see what my second surprise is." "Hold up, hold up! So he just paid for all this shit, gave you ten bands and he has more in store for you after this?" "Yea, that's right." I gave Redbone a slutty grin. "Yea, bitch, you gonna have to bust it open for a real nigga tonight." We all busted out laughing. "On the real, y'all think this shit too easy. I can get used to this lifestyle." "Don't get ahead of yourself, Choc, you barely know him." "I know, Redbone." "OK! I'm just saying, don't get it over your head, that's all." "Baby, this is me you talking to. I'm about my bread, and if he is spending it, we good.

After this store, I'm done with y'all cuz I can't hold shit else. My arms tired and feet hurting from all this walking. I'ma shoot Plug a text to send the ride." "OK! That's cool, but a bitch is starving." "What y'all wanna eat? We can get some wings or something from here. Let's just walk in that direction, so y'all can make y'all minds up. I'm ready to see what the rest of the night holds for me." "Bitch, he is probably about to take you to the spot and blow your brains out." "Wait, hoe, you tried it. Fuck! I look like fucking a nigga in a spot. If he just took us on this lavish ass shopping spree, I know he ain't gonna try me on no hoe shit like that. Stop hating." "Bitch, ain't nobody hating. I'm just stating facts." "Well, he might get the pussy, but it won't be in no spot! Damn, when you got so sensitive?" "Man, can both y'all shut the hell up! We can never go a full day without one of us arguing. I'm tired of hearing this shit." "Oh, we've pissed Redbone off, lol. Jalisa always starting shit." "Choc, you ain't making shit better; just let it go." "Yes, ma'am Redbone."

We ordered our wings and ate at one of the tables in the food court while we waited for Plug's errand boy to pull up. All I could think about was what my next surprise was going to be. I was anxious as hell and slightly nervous. "Aye, y'all! Our ride is outside; let's go." "OK! You taking the rest of these wings, Chocolate?" "Nawl, leave that shit on the table. Nasty ass." "Whatever, man, it's too much stuff in my hands." "See, Lee-Lee, yo ass always got something damn to say! I was talking to Raven. And I was talking to you bitch." "Hoe, you better be glad my hands are full." "Whatever, lol!" "Hey." "Hey. How y'all doing?

Who's getting dropped off first and where?" "Oh, we're all going to the same place." "Kool, say less. We dropped the girls off at Redbone's house, and I stayed in the car to get dropped off to my destination. The rest of the ride was silent and awkward. "Alright, we're here. Do you need me to help you with the bags?" "No, thanks. I can manage on my own." "Nawl, let me grab that for you. That nigga Plug would flip if he knew I let you struggle with all these bags." "If you insist." I handed him the bags I had in my hand, and he grabbed the rest from the trunk. We walked inside the Ritz Carlton. The lobby was so beautiful and fancy. Dude went straight to the elevator. "Aye, don't I need to check-in or something?" "Nawl, lil mama! I got the key for you in my pocket." "Oh, OK! Is it like that?" "Yea, I guess so." He dropped the bags at the door, handed me an envelope and walked away. I ripped open the envelope with so much excitement. Inside was instructions for what was about to take place. To my surprise, it was a nice negligee laid on the bed. It smelled so good like he sprayed it with perfume. I hurried to the restroom to shower. Singing my life away in the shower, I didn't hear my phone ringing. By the time I got out, the girls had called me 21 times. Frantically, I called back, hoping nothing was wrong. "Girl, Ma Sherry looking for you." "Well, what did y'all tell her?" "We told her you were with Keem." "Damn! Alright but I'm at the Ritz Carlton downtown if anything should happen." "What's the room number, Choc?" "We're in the penthouse, bitches!" "Oh, he got money, lol." "Girl, let me tell y'all. This nigga must do this for all his bitches cuz he left negligee for me to put on, flowers on the dresser, chocolate coved strawberries, and a bottle of champagne. It's about to be a good night!" "I bet it is, but yo ass better call Ma before she comes back down here looking for yo ass." "OK, y'all! I'ma call or text her and just say I'm spending the night with y'all." "Cool. Be safe, Chocolate, and have fun!" "OK! See y'all in the morning."

After sitting up in the bed for 2 hours, wondering when Plug's ass was gonna show up, I became restless and lay down. Somehow, I must have fallen asleep. I didn't hear the door open or anything, but when I opened my eyes there, he was sitting in a chair on the balcony. I slid the sliding door and joined him. "Hey, where were you?" I was bored all alone here. I had some business to handle. Sorry to keep you waiting, pretty lady." He grabbed my hand and kissed it. "Now come here and tell me about all the shit you got." I sat in his lap. "Let's talk about that later. I wanna show you how grateful I am." "Is that right?" he said as I slid down in front of him. Starring in his eyes, I pulled his Polo sweats down, just enough to whip his dick out. I kissed and licked the head of his penis until it was rock hard while looking up in his eyes. He licked his bottom lip and let his head tilt back slightly. Moaning, sucking and spitting all over his dick and jacking him at the same time. "You like that, Daddy?" "Yes, baby, can I cum on your face." "You can do whatever you like, baby." "Oh shit, girl, don't tell me that. You gonna make a nigga go crazy." I placed my index finger over his lips to silence him. He playfully bit it and sucked my finger as I pulled my hand from his grip. "Fuck, I'm about to cum, Choc!" I dropped my head back and held my tongue out as he stood up moaning and grunting loudly, and he jerked his dick, spraying cum all over my face. "Shit! Damn! Girl, who taught you that shit? Come on, so you can clean up." "I can't see, babe. Just get a rag so I can wipe these babies off my face." I licked my lips, and to my surprise, his nut didn't taste bad. He wiped my face and led me to the bed. Gently laying me on the edge of the bed, he spread my legs and scooped me up. I wrapped my legs around his neck as he raised me in the air. The warmth of his tongue sent chills up my spine. The way he was slurping and licking my pussy, you would've thought he was eating ice cream. "Awe yes, awe yes, I'm about to cum." "Yea, cum in my mouth, I wanna taste all of you." "It's coming, Daddy. Awe, fuck!" I exploded. My body still shivering from the orgasm. He laid me back on the bed. "Turn over, let me hit from the back so I can watch all this ass jiggle." I got on my knees and arched my back. He gently worked his penis inside my vagina. Tightly gripping my waist, the strokes got deeper and faster. The sound of him moaning with me made me wetter. He licked his thumb and stuck it in my butt. With every stroke, I could feel the urge to climax getting stronger and stronger. He pulled out and flipped me on my back. Aggressively pushing my legs back behind my head while he went face deep in my pussy. He came back up Backup, leaned in to kiss me. I sucked my juices off his bottom lip. Slowly, he inserted his penis back into my pussy. "Whose pussy this is?" "Yours! It's your pussy, Daddy." "Tell me it's mine!" "It's your pussy, babe." "Ugh! Shit. I'm about to cum, Choc." "Yes. Cum for me, Daddy!" "Awe, I'm coming, baby." "Yes, Daddy, cum." Plug let out a loud moan and lay on top of me. I just lay there for a minute, but his ass was heavy. "Babe, I need to get up." "OK! Fuck, girl, that lil pussy got some power. I gotta have you." I smiled and walked to the bathroom. I turned the shower on and motioned for Plug to join me. "Round 2, you ready?" "Damn, Choc, what you trying to do to me?" "Shhh! It'll be worth your while." I gently pushed him up against the wall. Slowly, I sucked from the head down to the shaft of his long, hard, girthy penis. I was trying to devour it as if it was my last meal. Only this time, I was careful not to leave his balls unattended. I gently massaged his balls while simultaneously sucking them too. With every moan he let out, the grip he had on my head got tighter and tighter. He was shoving his dick as far as he could in my mouth. Just when he was about to cum, I slowly pulled it out while giving him a slight grin. "I'm not ready for you to nut yet, Daddy" Plug forcefully pushed me against the shower door, tonguing me down and caressing my breast, sucking one at a time and rubbing my clitoris. My pussy was throbbing, and I was ready to feel him inside. I slowly lifted my left leg and inserted his dick inside me. This was a different feeling from the condom sex we just had. I was aroused on another level. The heat radiating from his manhood made my juices flow uncontrollably. "Damn, Choc! Yo young ass ain't playing! You gonna make a nigga wife you." All the while, the strokes were getting faster and longer. I was about to reach my climax. I sunk my teeth into his chest as he power-drove his dick inside me. With one motion, he turned and bent me over. I was grinding against his dick, trying to make it a night he was sure to remember. Plug pulled my hair, causing my head to tilt back, he leaned in to kiss me. We both orgasmed at the same time. After catching my breath, I turned around to look at him. He pulled me into his arms and just held me for a minute. The water from the overhead shower poured down on us like rain. We washed up and exited the bathroom. I was so tired. By the time my head hit the pillow, I was sound asleep.

The morning sun shining through the opening of the curtains caused me to wake up in a panic. I had slept longer than I originally planned. I walked through the room swiftly, looking for my belongings. I was in such a panic I didn't notice Plug was gone. My heart sort of jumped out of my body like, "Where the fuck is this nigga? Why didn't he wake me up when he left?" I was confused. I turned to the nightstand to grab the cellphone he brought me, and to my surprise, it was a note and a small gift bag on the dresser. The note read: "Thank you for a beautiful night. It was more than I ever imagined. I left a gift for you. I hope you like it. I'll see you soon." I laid the note down and opened the bag. It was a diamond tennis bracelet and 2 Plan B pills. I read the instructions and took the pills. What confused me the most was that he gave me 2 when the instructions said if taken properly, I would only need one pack. However, in Dre's directions, he told me to take on pack then and the other one the next day. I guess he wanted to be certain I didn't end up pregnant. Not that I was mad because I wasn't trying to get knocked up either. I was living my best life, and a baby would only interfere with that. I popped the pills and headed for the bathroom. While in the shower, I screamed and did my little happy dance! I knew I had won him over. I was ready to run his pockets dry. Startled by a knock at the door, I jumped out of the shower and grabbed the bathrobe off the hook. Very hesitantly, I walked over to the door. I looked out the peephole, and it was one of Dre's boys. I guessed he was there to take me home. "Hold on! I'm not dressed. Give me a sec." I threw on some sweats and went out the door. Unlike the first errand boy, this dude was all in my business. "So, what up?" "What's up?" "Nawl, I mean, like you wanna slide with me or you got other business to handle?" "What the fuck you mean by do I wanna slide with you?" "You trying to kick it or what?" "Nigga, you are an errand boy. Fuck, I look like sliding with you? I'm with the nigga that feeds you. What makes you think I want an underdog? You just fucking tried me!" "Nawl, chill, baby girl, I thought you were a trick. I didn't know it was like that." "Pussy nigga, you must not know who I am? My cousins will knock your block off talking to me out the side of yo neck. Pull over, let me out this fucking car!" "Man, bitch, chill! I'ma take yo ass home cuz Plug ain't gonna kill me cuz you wanna get in your feelings about a misunderstanding." "Nigga, I'ma tell Plug what you said to me." "Man, listen. It's not that deep. I thought this was something else. I apologize, ma!" "I'm not your ma! Just get me home so I can get out this fucking car." "Alright, shorty!" I couldn't wait to get out of the car. As we approached the apartments, I started grabbing my bags. I was so ready to get out the car with this rude, disrespectful nigga. "Say, ma, I mean Miss Lady, what I gotta do to keep this between you and me? Plug doesn't need to know about this lil mix-up." "Are you trying to fucking bribe me?" "Not really bribe you; just take it as an apology." "Kool, run it!" He handed me $1500. "Thanks! Nice doing business with you. Don't let it happen again." I slammed his car door and walked off.

Chapter Thirteen

Fast Pace

The girls and I were in the mall on the regular now. Only now we didn't have to steal the shit because I was the girlfriend of the Plug, literally. Lol, shit happened faster than I could blink. Originally, I was only supposed to talk to dude to get back at Jay. No way was my young ass supposed to be dating this twenty-four-year-old man. Sadly, Plug hadn't asked my age, and I never told him. In my mind, I thought he must know I was young cuz when we met, he was calling me on my momma's house phone. He was fed up with calling for me and Dj would lie and say I was outside with the girls or that he would tell me to call him back later. Plug pulled up to my school, beating down the block in his BMW Armored X5 SUV. He handed me a gift bag, and my insides filled with happiness! I leaned in and kissed his face all over in a full circle before I even looked at what was inside. I licked my lips and gave him a sly grin as I reached over to unzip his pants. Just as he was about to question my motives, I placed my finger over his lips. I didn't want him to ruin the moment. I reached in. pulling his semi-erect penis through his briefs. Slowly, I licked and sucked the head while he moaned and begged for me to deep throat all of him. Each time, I swallowed more and more of his dick. I could feel his grip get tighter, pulling my hair. The car started to swerve across the lane. I gagged and spat all over his dick, looking up in his eyes as I sucked it back off. I loved the sound of him moaning and calling my name underneath his breath. The throbbing of his dick in my mouth, the feeling of his veins against my tongue was making my pussy sing a tune of its own. I motioned for him to pull the car over as I slid my panties off. Before we could come to a complete stop, I was straddled across his lap. My juices dripped down his dick as I rubbed the head against my clitoris. I playfully stared into his eyes as I eased my way down on his shaft, trying to play off the fact that his dick was so big and thick. I breathed deeply with each stroke getting deeper and deeper. I could feel it in my guts, and all I could do was take all of it in. He slammed me into his hips as he was about to climax. His heavy breathing and loud moans made me want more and more of him. Just as I exploded, I could hear him say, "Fuck! I love you, girl!" but I ignored the notion and continued to push my hips into his as I finished my orgasm. I kissed his soft sweet lips and fell back into the seat. I could only imagine what was going through Plug's head because I thought I could get used to this. He probably wasn't thinking that our second sexual encounter would happen in the front seat of his car. I was trying to secure my spot and knock any bitch that might have thought they had a chance out of the running. "Damn, Choc, how many dicks have you sucked before me, girl? Those niggas were crazy to let you go! I'll give you everything I have if you keep sucking dick and fucking on sight like that." I smiled my shy grin, avoiding the first part of the question because it hadn't been many before him. I just heard enough of Lee-Lee's stories to know what needed to be done. "I'll have you to know that I'm not some hoe just out here sucking dick and fucking people all willie nillie. I've only been with one other person besides you." I rolled my eyes, pretending to be mad. "Girl, fix yo damn face, it was just a joke. But I hope yo ass knows you won't be sucking no more because that throat belongs to me now." "Wait! What? Now my throat belongs to you?" "You heard me right! That's a rap for these lame-ass niggas. You belong to me now." I smiled and said, "Whatever!" playfully. We pulled up to this fancy restaurant. I panicked and threw a fit about going in because I had on a school uniform and felt out of place. "If you would close your mouth for a second, you would know I had a change of clothes and shoes in your bag." I felt stupid because I had given this man the best of me and didn't even know if he deserved it or not. Shame on me. So, I climbed in the back seat and changed my clothes. I wanted badly to throw on some makeup, but Mr. Impatient was worried we would miss our reservations. We walked into the restaurant hand and hand. It was breathtaking. The ambience was spectacular. It was the perfect blend of exquisite and romance. Things got even better as we walked down to our tables, and we discovered that we got window seats where we had a beautiful view of the Chattahoochee River. The menu was a little out of my league, being that I'd never dined at such an upscale establishment. I let Plug order my food for me. The waiter even brought us over some expensive top-quality wine per Plug's request. I was almost afraid to drink any because I was underage for one but also because I didn't want Plug to get arrested. Reluctantly, I still took a few sips. I didn't want to drink too much because I knew what alcohol did to me. I needed the wine to curve my nerves because I was not sure if I was more nervous or scared. Plug could tell I was out of my comfort zone. "Aye, Chocolate, let's go down by the water for a minute." "What about when the man brings our food?" "It'll be OK. I just wanna show you something." I took the cloth napkin that I placed on my lap, and sat it at the edge of the table, pushed my chair back, and Plug grabbed my hand to lead me to the door. The air smelled fresh, and the breeze was cool, coming off the water. We held hands and just walked in silence for a moment before Plug started to laugh. I looked at him to see what was funny. His eyes were fixed on the water. "Did I miss the joke?" "Chill, lil baby, it's no joke but why the hell your hand shaking so bad?" "Hush!" I said as I playfully pushed him toward the water. "I'm nervous for one, my momma gonna nut up when I get home, and secondly, I've never been to a restaurant like this before. This is beyond anything I could imagine." "Well, get used to it, punk. If you play yo cards right, you'll have plenty more dates like this." The waiter signaled to us that our food was ready. We walked back to our table and enjoyed our meal. "Tonight is definitely going down in my book as the best night ever. I know it may seem foolish and too soon but, on the way, I am making plans to be this nigga's wife in my head." All I could think about was all the foolish bitches that let him slip away. Currently, I didn't know how I would keep him, but I knew I wanted to have him all to myself!

As we approached the apartments, I was brought back to reality, and I knew Momma was about to preach my damn head off about respect and trying to be grown before my time. I didn't care much, but I wanted her to feel as though I did, out of respect. I tried to prepare my mind for the shit while thinking how jealous the girls were going to be when I would tell them about the lavish ass date Plug took me on. The car came to a stop, and my nerves were raging again. "Alright, lil mama! I'll catch you later." "Damn! That's how you gonna dismiss me?" "Listen, baby, to you I'm a gentleman, but in these streets, I'm a thug. I have an image I have to maintain." "So, you too hard to give a bitch a hug?" "Nawl, baby, it's not like that, but if you gonna be my lady, you gotta respect this shit." "Kool, say no more." Plug could tell I had an attitude, but he didn't try to stop me from getting out the car. I hoped he would come behind me and try to put an end to the childish tantrum I was throwing, but he drove off.

Chapter Fourteen

Wrong Turn

Things with Plug and me were moving at rapid speed. I was excited and scared all at once. Only thing I was certain of was that I needed to be on birth control. After landing myself at the abortion clinic, yet another time, I refused to do that shit again! Only this time, Plug sat there with me instead of Kim. All the grown bitches from the apartments were all in my business, and I just knew the shit was gonna get back to my momma. I tried to lie low with my Armani Exchange hoodie over my head, but as usual, this nigga had to make shit about him. "What? You ashamed to be in here with a nigga or something?" "What the hell are you talking about?!" "And why you so damn loud? "This isn't about you! This shit is just embarrassing altogether! I know one of these nosy ass hoes gonna go tell my momma they saw me up in here, and I don't have time for this shit." "I'll go talk to Mama and throw her a few racks for some Sunday suits and hats. She'll be OK." Plug laughed. I didn't find the shit funny, but instead of arguing and further embarrassing myself, I just sat there quietly, waiting for my name to be called. It really pissed me off that his ugly ass thought that money could fix every-damn-thing! If this shit got out, my mom and grandma would be devastated. It wasn't the Christian thing to do, and our family didn't believe in abortions. Unbeknownst to them, here I was my second time, riding this rodeo. At that moment, I promised I would never step foot in that place again. I got on birth control and made Plug ass pull out from that day on! He thought he was gonna keep nutting in me then throw them lousy ass four hundred dollars at me like he was some fucking abortion fairy, throwing fairy dust or some shit.

I was losing focus like hell. Missing school and falling asleep in class, having been out all night with Plug. In my mind, I knew I needed to break shit off with him if I had any plans of going to college still. Or graduating for that matter cuz shit was all bad for me. I knew Lee-Lee and Redbone were so fucking mad at me because I swore to them I had this shit under control. In all honesty, shit was getting too far out of hand. Plug ass had me lying to every damn body that cared anything about my ass. Keeping secrets from my best friends, missing important shit in Shante's and Dj's lives, and hell, I was missing shit in my own life. He thought all my time belonged to him. I won't front like I wasn't enjoying all the lavish gifts, vacations and shit that came with the lifestyle, but I was only seventeen and still lived with my damn momma. Out here wilding, acting like I was grown or some shit. Momma didn't mind because, with all the missed time, she was compensated well for it. Hell, Plug even took us all on family vacations. In Momma's eyes, he couldn't do no wrong. She thought he was prince charming. If only she knew. And NO, he wasn't beating on me or nothing but that surely as hell didn't stop him from calling me every name but the name my momma gave me when he was mad. I remember sitting in this upscale restaurant all the way in Italy when I fucked around and smiled at the waiter far too long for his liking. "Bitch, you think I brought you halfway around the world for you to be smiling at this nigga like you stupid or some hoe? I'll flip this motherfucker upside down you ever disrespect me like that!" "Babe, calm down! I was only thanking the man for his services." "Don't fucking tell me to calm down!

Hoe, you think I care about these fucking folks looking at us?" "Oh, let me guess; I'm embarrassing you, huh?" "No, babe, you're not. Can we just go, please?" "Nawl, I'm not done eating. We'll leave when I'm done. How about that, bitch?" I silently got up and excused myself to the restroom. I looked at the girl in the mirror laced in jewelry and designer clothes but unhappy as hell. I wanted so bad to storm out there and smack the shit out of him, but I was too far from home to call the girls for a ride. I got myself together and walked back toward the table. The table was empty. To my surprise, Plug had left me. I ran outside, and the valet worker said he called for the car and left. He spoke a little bit of English, so he helped me call a cab. Before I got back to the room, I had plenty of time to think during the ride. I was sick of Plug's shit. I pushed the door open and instantly started going off! "I don't know who the fuck you think I am, but I'm done tolerating your disrespectful bullshit! I have never ever given you a fucking reason to distrust me!! I'm more loyal to you than your so-called friends and punk ass workers! You treat them motherfuckers better than you treat me! I'm tired of this shit, Dre!" He hit the mute button on the TV and stood up. All the nerves in my body were in shock. I didn't know what to expect, but I was ready for whatever. I was fucking fed up. Plug walked over to me and grabbed my face. In my head, I envisioned him squeezing my head until it popped. Instead, he kissed me and apologized over and over. "Baby, I'm sorry. I promise I'll never talk to you like that ever again." I had heard that shit time and time again. "Dre, you always say that shit, so I don't leave, and you think cuz you take me shopping or leave stacks of dough on the dresser that it is supposed to fix it every time. I'm tired of trying to prove my love to you. Look at me! I could have whatever a man I want, but I chose you! I choose to be here with you, and you wanna fight. I can't do this anymore. I'm tired of it." I sat at the edge of the bed with a face full of tears and so many thoughts in my head. I heard a deep sigh, and the door slammed shortly. I thought he would return and try to charm his way back in, but not this time. Shockingly, I was OK with that, though. I didn't know how I would get home, but it didn't even matter. I stayed for the remainder of the days we had left on our vacation so that I could gather my thoughts. The girls might have called me a thousand times, but I knew they were calling to be nosy. I wasn't in the mood to talk about it right now. I was sad and heartbroken. I would explain it all once I got back home. By every second from the last day, I was done sapping and throwing myself a pity party. I was enjoying the city of love and my solitude. I had come up with a master plan to keep up the lifestyle that I had become accustomed to. Who knew how much foreigners loved black women. The guy that cost me my relationship stopped me while at the market and offered me ten bands to fly over here once a month just to see him. Hell, who said the business couldn't be a vacation as well. I even told him I would have to bring my girls if I came back. He was OK with that, now all I had to do was come up with a way to get their ass out of Georgia. Knowing them, they wouldn't turn down a free vacation. I knew Jalisa would be in on this money move, so it wouldn't take much to convince her. Raven, on the other hand, wouldn't want no part in this shit. I tried to sleep, but sleep wasn't my friend. I couldn't help but think of what type of drama I would be walking back into once I reached the states. I knew Plug wouldn't let me walk away easily. I almost lost sight of who I was, but all I needed was a reminder.

On the plane ride home, I drew out my money plan. If Jalisa was down to take a few clients, I would take a cut of her money and pay myself for setting up all the meetings. I planned to talk about the money move before I got into the drama between Plug and me. I was hyped getting off the plane as I strutted down to baggage claims. I had my earbuds in my ear, so I didn't hear nor did I notice the gang of people following me with dozens and dozens of flowers. Some strange man tapped my shoulders to get my attention. I let out a scream. "Oh, my! I didn't mean to startle you. You are Sheri, right?" "It depends on who wants to know." "Well, my team and I were hired to bring you these bags and all these flowers." "Well, take them back and tell him I said I'm good." "Why? Yes, madam, I will." "Thanks," I said as I placed my earbuds back in and grabbed my luggage. This nigga Dre had some nerves. For some strange reason, as I approached the door, my heart started to race. Just like my gut was telling me that Dre was outside waiting for me and told the girls they could leave that he would take me home. "What the fuck, Plug?" "Baby, let me explain." "There's no need to explain. I'm tired of this shit. You think because I'm young, you can dog me and treat me any kind of way? I have fucking feelings, Plug, and the way you talk to me is out of pocket!" "I know, baby, but I love you. I can't let you walk away. Choc, you got my head fucked up. I can't eat or think straight without you." "Well, the way you be carrying on, I can't tell." "Damn, baby, you gonna keep bitching or you gonna let me show you how sorry I am?" "Yea, I guess." I couldn't help but smile. The nigga was fine as fuck, and I couldn't resist his beautiful brown eyes and his pearly whites. Yea, I was a sucker, but I was a paid sucker. We pulled up to a house I had never been to. "Whose house is this, Dre?" "Why you gotta ask questions? Just unbuckle yourself and get out." My mind couldn't help but wonder. However, I refrained from asking any more questions. As we walked to the door, I noticed rose petals everywhere and the door opened on its own. This shit was fancy. I smiled from ear to ear as Momma would say. The lights were dim, and everywhere smelled like heaven, even the air was nice and cool. Plug held my hand and led me out to the patio. Before we got to the opening, I could hear the music playing. "Babe this is so beautiful. A live band?" The water in the pool was the bluest blue I had seen. I was in awe at the scenery. Plug pulled a chair from the table and shortly after, a gentleman, dressed in a black and white suit, came to the table and poured us both some wine. Plug had outdone himself this time. A different server came to take our orders, and the menu was elegantly put together. I ordered the brown sugar garlic lamb, mashed potatoes, asparagus, and dinner rolls. We ate and stared at each other with very few words in between. I wondered what Plug had up his sleeves next, but I was just enjoying the moment. This was hella nice. Just as I was finished with my food, the kind server offered us some dessert. Plug smiled and said, "I'll be having this lovely lady for dessert." I laughed and passed up on the dessert as well. To my left, I could see a short lady approaching us as Plug motioned for me to stand. The lady grabbed my hand and led me to a room with a huge shower and a table set up for a massage. The shower floor was filled with pink and red rose petals and candles all around the base. I bathed and laughed and breathed in all the loveliness of this strange place I was in. I walked back to the table where the short Asian lady awaited me. Slowly, I climbed on the table and lay down. The oil she drizzled all over my body smelled like sweet cinnamon. The warmth of her hand grazing across my bare naked skin made my pussy moisten. The whole inside of my body tingled. I had never had this type of feeling with a woman touching me. I closed my eyes and imagined that she was about to take me to ecstasy. Suddenly, the feel of the hands changed. Now it was a stronger touch, and I could feel his breath on the back of my neck. I moaned at the thought of two people pleasing me. Warm lips against the bottom of my foot. Slowly, I felt them creeping higher and higher up my leg. The grip on my hips tightened and became more intense. On the inside of my thighs more kisses. I spread my legs wider to make way to the sweet juices that were now flowing out of my dripping wet pussy. Afraid to open my eyes, I slowly turned onto my back. The Asian lady grabbed my hands and led me to a rose petal filled circular bed in the middle of the patio right outside of the bedroom. Kissing me so passionately as we lay down on the bed. Down to my neck, she placed wet kisses until she was in between my legs. Dre caressed his hard-erect penis as he walked over to the bed. The sexy Asian sucked and tongue-kissed my pussy one last time and walked away. Dre picked up right where she left off. I was on a high. The feeling of bare skin at the entryway of my pussy instantly caused my hips to move in a grinding motion. I wanted so bad to feel him inside of me. He teased me as I begged for him to beat his pussy up. Finally, I had had enough. I took the tip of my foot, pushing him down onto the bed. He was going to beat this pussy up when I said it and how I said it. I instructed him to get on his knees and eat it as if his life depended on it. Gripping the back of his head, I ground my hips into his face. Just as I was about to explode, I pushed him back and climbed on top of him. Grabbing the whip off the table next to the bed, I struck him. Not hard but just enough to let him know that I was in charge now. I rode him like a cowgirl riding to victory. "Say my name! Who's the boss?!" "You are, baby! You're the boss!" I slammed my hips into him. "I'm cumin, Sheri; I'm cumin!" I jumped off and stared into his eyes just long enough to let the urge to nut die down just a little before I took his hard penis into my mouth. I sucked and licked his balls and slid my hands up and down his penis. Slowly kissing the tip as I looked at him, begging me to suck it and let him bust in my mouth. I wasn't ready for it to be over. Plug aggressively sat up and playfully slung me on to my back. He tongue fucked me so hard and stuck his thumb in my butt. Just as I was about to cum, my moans intensified, and he shoved his penis inside of me. I gasped for air and at the same time we both exploded and just lay in the pool of juices beneath us.

Chapter Fifteen

Money Moves

Playtime was over. I had to regain my focus and get to this bag. I know if Plug ever found out he would probably kill me. I had to be extra careful if my little sting operation was going to work. I called Lee-Lee up to go to the wing spot so I could hip her to the game. "Hey, Lee-Lee!" "What's up, Choc?" "Girl, nothing, but I may have a money move for you. Let's hit to wing spot so we can chat." "Damn, Choc, I can't go right now." "Cool, but you don't wanna miss this money train." "Can you come to the house to chop it up?" "I really don't want Ma to hear us talking about it cuz, to be honest, dawg, I don't know how we gonna pull this off. It's so much money to be made, though, so we gotta work this shit out." "My mama is not here, which is really why I can't leave the house right now. She lost the damn door keys again, drinking at the bar on 5th street." "Cool, say no more." As I walked to Jalisa's house, I was already looking for flights because we needed to head out as early as possible on Friday. I also wanted to be certain that nothing in this planning would fail through the cracks. Gabriel had the room booked. All I had to do was be sure that Lee-Lee was down for the ride, which I knew she would be. I turned the knob to Jalisa's front door and went in. "Lee-Lee, where you at?" "I'm in the bathroom. Just go to the room; here I come." Call me crazy, but it sounded like she was in there fucking. The sound of her voice was winded and shaky. I minded my own business and went straight to the room. About five minutes later, she came out smiling, looking crazy. "Bitch, I know you're not crazy enough to be fucking in your mom's house! What if it was her coming in and not me." "Man, I knew it was you. She won't be home for at least another hour, but what's up? What was so damn important?" "OK! So, I know I didn't tell y'all, but Plug and I got into it in Italy and he left me. That's why he got home before me. Before you interrupt me, I'm not here to talk about that shit. While I was there, this server stopped me and asked if I was interested in making some major bread. So, he said he'd pay me 10 bands and pay for all flights and hotel stays if I slept with him. As it turns out, they love black women over there. I don't wanna do this shit alone, and it's plenty of money for both of us to make a killing." "Bitch, are you trying to prostitute me?" "Man, hell nawl! I'm just trying to include you so you can make some money. I respect it if you don't want to do it. But look at it this way, you are around here, fucking and sucking for free! We can go to a country where no one knows us, fly straight in and do what we gotta do and bring our ass back home. If we do this every weekend, you know how much money we can bring in? I'm talking 110,000 by the end of summer." "Man, Chocolate, that's a lot of money! How we gonna go without telling our parents? I don't even have a passport." "Don't worry about that. I know a dude who can get you one under the table." "Cool. Run it!" "See! That's why you re my bitch. I knew you would be down. We can't tell Raven that we doing this. Even if she goes with us, she can't know what we're doing. You know she would flip on us." "Yea, she'll probably call us all kinds of hoes, lol." "I'm about to tell Gabriel it's a go."

Headed for the airport, Jalisa was worried about her passport. I kept trying to get her to be cool so that she didn't draw attention to us. Finally, we made it through TSA and was boarding our plane.

Once our plane landed, Gabriel was waiting for us at the gate. We didn't bring Redbone this time because we had to see how this was going to play out. We went straight to the hotel to check in and freshen up. Gabriel waited in the living area of our suite. "OK, Lee-Lee, all we have to do is put on these Nun customs and go out there and give him a show." "Chocolate, I can't believe we're doing this." "Listen, don't think about the shit. Just picture yourself at home in your mirror dancing. Let him touch you a lil bit, and it'll be over before you know it. Here, drink this shot of Hennessy, it'll ease your nerves." "Bitch, you acting like you're a pro at this. Let me find out you been out here tricking off." "It's not tricking; it's escorting!" "Whatever!" "Put your glass in the air. Cheers to new money!" We threw the shot back and poured another. Drank it and walked out the bathroom. To my surprise, Gabriel was still alone. I side-eyed Lee-Lee because I and this nigga wasn't trying to have a threesome. That was going to cost him extra. I didn't tell Lee-Lee because I was going to pocket the extra money, which I was going to ask for. I walked out before Lee-Lee because I knew she was nervous. "Alright, Gabriel, I heard you've been a naughty boy. It's spanking time." Gab bent over for me to paddle him for being a bad boy. I apologize Sister Mary. Now, put that pussy in my face." As told, Lee-Lee very shyly spread her legs like an eagle while Gabriel went down, slurping all of her juices. I spanked him harder. Made her moan louder. I instructed him on what to do. I knew he wanted to see some girl on girl action, so I stood over Lee-Lee who at first looked at me with a crazy look. I kissed her soft juicy lips as Gabriel looked up with approval. "Sister Mary, I want you to feast on Sister Ann's pussy." I felt my body curl, and vomit welled up in my throat, but I knew this would be our secret. I sat on Lee-Lee's face before she had time to process what was about to happen. Grinding my hips into her face, I could feel Gabriel's hand on my ass. "Spank me. Awe, yes!" I moaned in ecstasy. The sound of paper rattling and moans getting louder. I sucked my pussy juices from Lee-Lee's lips. Gabriel was obsessed with her smooth dark chocolate skin. "Sister Mary, bend over, and Sister Ann, put your pussy in my face." I was in shock at the way he was fucking Lee-Lee with so much aggression and equally devouring my pussy. Lee-Lee reached up and started rubbing my clitoris. I had never had 2 people pleasing me at once, but I loved every bit of it. The orgasm I experienced was like no other. Gabriel didn't fuck me this time and that was OK. The plane ride home was so fucking awkward. Neither one of us said much. However, I knew we had to discuss what took place, so I broke the silence. "Listen, Jalisa, I know that wasn't part of the plan, but shit, this gotta be our secret. If Redbone or anyone ever found out, it would be crazy." She didn't respond at first. I knew she was processing all that shit, and it was a lot to take in. "Shari, you're my best friend, like my fucking sister. The closest thing I have to a sister. There's no way that shit is happening again. You better tell your people we not doing no threesomes cuz next time, I'ma walk on your ass." "OK! Deal! I love you." I handed her $15,000 and kept the other $15,000.

Chapter Sixteen

Judgment

The next day after we returned to the city, I went to have lunch with Redbone without Jalisa. My phone was ringing all night with people trying to set up appointments. I needed someone to handle that part of the operations. I was reluctant to involve her at first because I didn't want her to judge the journey we were on. I knew she wouldn't be cool with it, and she probably was going to have a lot of shit to say about it, but she was the only person that I trusted to handle this. I sat at the table waiting for her to walk in. I was nervous and somewhat scared. I felt a tap on my shoulder and turned around. It was Plug. I was cursing like hell in my head because I wasn't expecting to see him. "Hey, babe. What are you doing here? You spying on me?" "Don't babe me when I was calling your ass all night and you didn't answer the fucking phone." "Babe, calm down. I fell asleep and didn't put my phone on the charger. I apologize." "Yea, alright. Don't make me beat your ass, Chocolate." "Babe, I promise. Give me a kiss. I miss you." "Yea, I hear you. Why the fuck you in here by yourself?" "I'm waiting for Redbone's slow ass so we can eat." "Oh, OK! Well, I'ma get out your way. I gotta go make a play, but I better see you later or we gonna have a real situation." "I don't want no beef, babe. Lol, I'll call you later." I was shaking in my fucking bones. I wasn't expecting to see his ass so soon. Few minutes later, Redbone's slow ass came strolling in. "Hey, Chocolate." "What's up, Redbone? I need to talk to you about something really important." "OK! What's up? I'm all ears for about an hour." "Cool! So Lee-Lee and I have this lil business, and we need you to book the flights and run our schedules. I'ma buy this flip phone and, when they call to set the appointments, you just have to find an open weekend, take their card information to pay for the hotel and flights. Once you have booked the flights and room, call them back with the confirmation." "Wait! What the fuck type of business y'all hoes running. Open legs happy hour special or some shit?!" "Lol, hell yea, if you put it like that. Matter of fact, that's what I'ma call the shit." "Y'all bitches wild, man." "I mean, it's good money, Raven. I can get you some clients too if you wanna make some hard core cash." "Man, hell nawl! I can't sell my body." "I mean shit, at least, we get paid for some shit you gonna do anyway with a broke ass nigga that can't even buy you a dollar burger when he's done fucking you." "I get that, Choc, but I just can't see myself doing that shit. I can make the appointments and go with y'all, but that's it." "Cool! That's all I need you do. So now that that's out the way, how much you hoes paying me to be y'all personal assistant?" "I can pay you two thousand a week." "Bitch, say what?! Two thousand just to answer the phone and book flights? How much money y'all making?" "Last weekend, we made $15,000 just to dress up in some costumes to fulfill a nigga's fantasy." "That's wild, son. I can't believe y'all are actually doing this shit." "Listen, baby, I'ma get out the hood one way or another. I'm sick of living in the projects. Watch, I'ma make so much money, and I'ma buy my momma a house." "I hear you, Choc."

Gabriel spread the word fast. His friends, co-workers, neighbors, and everyone were calling, trying to get on the schedule. I didn't know business was gonna be booming like this, and I sure as hell didn't know how Lee-Lee and I were gonna handle all the clients, just the two of us. But we were booked to go to Cuba. It was a turnaround trip. I had to charge more since we wouldn't have time to enjoy ourselves after our work was done. Zeek thought that he would be getting a two for one special, but he was sadly mistaken. I booked Lee-Lee for him, and I took his friend. We had three separate rooms, although he wanted to have one big ass orgy. Lee-Lee had made it perfectly clear that she wasn't down with that shit no more. Soon as the tall, muscular guy entered the room, I was ready for business. He wanted to shower before we started. I patiently waited at the edge of the bed. I could hear the shower water stop. So, I tossed back an X-pill and prepared for the ride. As he walked over to me, the smile on his face was creeping me out. "What the hell is he so happy about?" I wondered. He dropped the towel. I had never seen a dick so big before. I took a deep breath. He grabbed his dick and instructed me to get on my knees. It was not only long but the width on that thang, I was unsure if I would be able to fit it all in my mouth. On all fours, I crawled over to him. He grabbed the leash that was attached to the choker on my neck and walked me in two full circles as I purred like a cat. The guy lay on the floor as I lifted my leg to pee on him. I had never given anyone a golden shower before but the enjoyment it gave him made my insides dance.

Chapter Seventeen

Love and War

(Fast forward)

"Choc, where you at?" frantic Raven yelled so loudly through the phone. I could barely understand her. "I'm down here with Jalisa picking up this money from... wait, what the hell wrong with you, Redbone?!" "Where you at?!" "B-shot bitch ass just jumped on me because I cursed one of his bitches out! Can you please come pick Aiden and me up?" "Yeah, we on the way and tell B-shot he better have his ass outta there before I get there!" "Okay, I'ma pack the baby stuff. Can yawl please hurry up?!" "We coming, baby! We're coming." Jalisa and I ran to the car and flew down the street to Raven's house. I hated the way Brian treated her. Raven was such a good person. B-shot was a big-time drug dealer on the Westside. Redbone met him when we were in the eleventh grade. He was buying her all kinds of lavish things. Damn, nearly every day, they were going shopping. He even brought her a car for twelfth grade graduation. B-shot was a big hoe though. He tricked off on all the young hoes in all the local projects. Everywhere we went, some chick wanted to fight Raven because of his ass! As Jalisa and I pulled up, we could hear Raven screaming at B-shot along with cries from the baby. I grabbed the gun that Plug brought me and ran up to the house. The door was already open, so we busted in. "B-shot, you better keep yo motherfucking hands off my sister!" "Man, yo sister better keep her ass in her place! She already knows what the deal is, so she needs to respect that shit man." Jalisa shot back, "What the fuck you mean respect some shit?! You better keep them lil young whores in check, fuck you mean! This is the mother of your fucking son, and you up in here fighting her for your side bitches?! You better motherfucking respect her. Hell are you talking about!" "She ain't gotta keep taking this shit from you! She's too damn pretty to be letting you fuck up her face and shit! Before I see you keep hurting her, I'll kill you, Brian!! You understand me?" I asked. "That's a fucking promise, not a threat! I love her to death, B-shot, you hear me?" "Choc, you ain't gonna come up in my shit, threatening me!" "It's not a threat, B; it's a fucking promise!" A promise huh Choc? "You fucking right it's a promise. B-shot, you not gonna be fighting her in front of our nephew no more! Jalisa and Choc, let's just go, get me away from here, please! I don't ever wanna see your ass again, Brian!" "What the fuck you mean, bitch?! Long as you got my motherfucking son, I'll be around! You can believe that, bitch! So, don't act in front of these bitches; you'll be back! You can't survive without me. You don't even have a job." "Fuck you, Brian! I gotta do what's right for my son! So, from here on, fuck you and everything you stand for, B-shot! You can have them nothing ass project hoes you've been fucking." At that moment Raven walked out the house. We all agreed the safest place for her to go was my house since B-shot had no idea where I lived. Thus, he couldn't come after her. We were careful to make sure one of his foot soldiers did not follow us. Once in the house, I put Raven and Aiden's stuff in the guest room of my house and returned to the living room with the girls to get the full story on what happened. We tried for hours to get Raven to calm down and stop crying, but it was an epic failure. "Redbone, you've been sitting in here, crying for two days. You need to get yourself together, if not for yourself, do it for the damn baby. I understand you love him and all, but he's not good for you, Red! You're too pretty for him to be beating you and bringing you all kinds of STDs and shit! I hate to say it, but the way Brian has been sleeping with the project chicks, he is going to give you something you can't get rid of! You have a son to live for. It's not just about you anymore. You have to do what's best for the baby and that type of living is not safe for Aiden." "I know, Choc, but I love him so much! He was my first everything!" "He might be your first everything, but, Red, don't let him be your last, and I mean by letting him kill you. I don't know what we would do without you." "I know what you mean, Sheri, and I'm not going back this time. He hit me while I had my baby in my hand; he really doesn't give a fuck about us." "Exactly, Redbone! So, think about it, Raven, and make the right decision for Aiden. Fuck love and love the love that truly loves you." "What am I supposed to do now, Sheri? I don't have a job, or anywhere to go. He's not gonna leave the house." "What the hell you mean, Raven?! You know you can stay here long as you need to, and you know I'll help you with the baby! Yawl are my family, and I be damned if I see you hurt or on the streets, you know that, Redbone. Now go clean yourself up and put some clothes on. We're about to have a girl's day." "Okay, but who's going to keep Aiden? Momma is at work, and I can't let Ms. Ruby keep him because she'll let B-shot get my baby with his stupid ass." Raven burst into tears. "Stop crying, Red, I'll call Shante, and she'll do it for a lil change. I got you, okay?" "Okay, Choc." "Now, go take yo ass a shower and get dressed, Jalisa B will be here in a minute, and you know that bitch can be impatient." "Okay, I love you, Sheri, you know, that right?" "Of course, Raven Redbone Smith! We're sisters, bitch; you better love me," I said, wrapping my arms around her. We both laughed and walked in different directions of the house. I looked back in relief just at the thought that she was smiling. Then there was a knock. "Raven, what the hell you in there doing? It doesn't take an hour to bathe! Red? Redbone you in there?!" "Choc, she's not answering! Redbone, answer me girl!" "Redbone, this is Choc! You better answer us, or we gonna kick this bitch in!! Stop playing and answer us!" "Oh, my God, Choc, what has she done?" Jalisa asked as we both stepped back to kick the door. We could tell she had her body against the door, and we were unsure of what was wrong, so we were scared but a decision had to be made. We kicked the door down and Raven was lying on the floor. "Call 911, Sheri! Call 911! Hurry up, please!!" "911 operator, what's your emergency?" "My, my, my sister! She's not breathing, she is not breathing, oh, my God! She's not breathing!" "Okay, ma'am, calm down! Where is your sister now?" "She's on the bathroom floor. Please send the paramedics, please! Hurry up, don't let my sister die, please! She was supposed to be taking a shower! She's not breathing! Send someone, please!" "Ma'am, calm down, so I can get the police and fire department out to your location. I need to ask you a few questions, is that okay?" "Yes, please just help us!" "Do you know how long she's been unconscious?" "No! She's been in the shower for about forty-five minutes to an hour. Can you please just send us some help?" "Raven, wake up, wake up! Please, just wake up! Choc, she is not getting up. Choc, what are we gonna do?! Redbone, please don't leave us like this, baby, you gotta wake up! Man, Red, get up please!" (Aiden crying in the background) "Choc, go get the baby! He's crying," Jalisa said crying and rocking Redbone's breathless body in her arms. "He can cry, it's not gonna hurt him. They need to come on, man!" "Raven, your baby needs you, please get up please! Jalisa, we gotta save her we can't let her die in the bathroom!" (Knocking) "Come In! We're back here, please hurry up!" "Grab a towel so I can cover her up, Choc! Hurry, sir, we're in the bathroom, just come straight back!" "Excuse me, move out the way please. Just give us space to work." They rushed Raven out to the truck, hooked her up to all kinds of machines and asked which one of us was riding with her. "I'll ride in the truck!" "No, Jalisa, you ride with her, and I'll follow yawl. Give me the baby. Hurry, hop in!" I hopped in my car and turned my emergency lights on. They went through every red light, and I was right behind them! Once we got to the hospital, the emergency team was already waiting at the door for them to bring Raven in. The paramedics pulled the stretcher out the ambulance and rushed through the doors. Jalisa and I were right behind them. "Ma'am, you can't come in here. I'm sorry. Please, wait right here in the family room. The doctor will be out with the news." "Okay, please save my sister, please!" Jalisa grabbed me, and we just held on to each other for a while, crying while Aiden looked at us with confusion on his face. "They're going to do everything they can, ma'am." Jalisa snapped back, "She needs one of us with her; she needs to know we're here!" "Ma'am, I understand that but if you want the doctors to save her, you must allow them time and space to do their jobs." "Jalisa, calm down! She knows we're here; she knows that. We can't go in there. We have to let them folks do their jobs. Calm down, please. We need to call her mom, Jalisa; we gotta call Ms. Lisa! She doesn't even know about the fight or none of this shit." "Sheri, what are we going to tell her, man? This shit is fucked up!" "That's not important. We'll tell her something once she gets here! Just tell her to get here ASAP!" "Hello?" "Hey, Ms. Lisa! This is Jalisa, um we're here at the hospital with Raven." "What? What's wrong with my baby? That no good baby daddy of hers did something to my child?!" "Ms. Lisa, it's very important that you get here as soon as possible." "Okay, Jalisa baby, I'm on the way. I'm on my way!" Her voice trembled. I could tell she was about to break down. "Choc, you need to sit down before you have a nervous breakdown or walk a hole in the floor." "I can't! If she dies on me, Jalisa, I'ma kill B-shot! Look at what he has done to our sister! She's only twenty-five years old, man. She's too young to die. She gotta make it for her son, man!" "I know, Sheri. I know! Just come sit down. Stop crying, baby. God will bring her through this, I know He will. Let's just pray and wait!" After about five or ten minutes everybody in Raven's family started pouring in. I didn't even know how to tell them that Raven did this to herself. "Ms. Lisa, we're over here." "Sheri and Jalisa, what happened to my baby? What did he do to her this time?" "Well, to be honest, he's not the direct cause this time, not the way you're thinking. Sit down, Ma, let me explain. Jalisa and I were out running some errands when Raven called, yelling and pleading for us to come pick her and the baby up. B-shot jumped on her because Raven cursed some chick out he supposed to be messing with." "I told that child to leave that boy alone! He has messed up my baby's whole life! Raven was a smart girl! Now she's lying up in this damn hospital, and we don't know if she's dead or alive!" "I know, Ms. Lisa, but I promise I'll take care of B-shot. I know it won't make things right, but it'll make me feel better!" "Excuse me! Can the immediate family of Raven Smith please come follow me; the doctor will speak to you now." Ms. Lisa, Raven's dad, sister, his side of the family, Jalisa and I all went to a different waiting room. "Lord, please just let my child make it. She's my only child. I can't lose her like this. Please, Lord, save my baby!" "Hey, I'm Dr. Jefferson." "Hi!" "I was the one working on Ms. Smith. She's going to be okay! We had to do a lot of work on her, so she's going to be in here for a while." "Thank you, doctor! Thank you for saving my child. Thank you, Lord. Lord, have mercy, thank you!" "I don't know what happened, but she had a few broken ribs and bruises. Seems like she ingested some pills and then slightly drowned. So, we will have her under close watch to make sure there is no brain damage. You'll be able to see her in a few hours." "Okay, thank you so much, Doctor Jefferson." "Jalisa, I gotta go handle some things. I'll be back in a few hours. Where are my keys?" "Where you going, Choc? Don't do this tonight. Let's just go home and get some rest." "I'll take you home, but I gotta do this, Jalisa. That nigga almost just killed my sister!" "I know! Damn it! She's my sister too, Sheri, but you don't need to go out there tonight looking for him! Just go home and get some rest, please!" "Ugh! Okay! Okay! But I'ma go holler at Bj and his boys tomorrow. B-shot gonna get his! Let me see if Ms. Lisa wants Aiden, or he's going back to the house with me." "Okay, I'll be sitting in the car." "Ms. Lisa, we're going home to get some rest. Do you want us to take Aiden home or you're taking him with you?" "Nawl, baby, I'm staying down here all night, you know, in case something goes wrong." "I understand. Well, we're all staying at Chocolate's house, so call us if you should need anything or if things go wrong." "Okay, baby! And thanks for being such good friends to my baby, you hear?" "Yes, ma'am, you're welcome!"

"Choc, you need to lie down! Pacing the floor all night isn't going to change things." "I know, but I just feel like Brian's ass almost killed my sister, and he needs to pay." "Do you hear yourself, Sheri? Almost, baby; she's not dead, so just let it go. Don't go trying to get revenge and throw your whole life away. What sense does that make? Hell, she might get out and go back to the nigga, and you are out here getting yourself into trouble. You have a career. You don't need to throw it all away on a low life nothing ass nigga like B-shot. Is his ass worth all the long nights you stayed up studying and stressing, trying to get through college?" "Nawl, his low life nothing, but Raven is!" "Choc, you gotta be smart in this situation." "I'm being smart, Jalisa! That's why I'm not doing it. My hands are gonna be clean of the whole situation. I'm not gonna put that tag on his head just yet because it'll be too obvious." "Don't do it at all, Choc! He's still Aiden's father even if we don't want him to be. You know how it felt growing up without a father. You hated your mom for killing your dad." "Yeah, I know, but I want him to feel the pain he's causing my best friend." "You want Aiden to grow up hating his aunt for killing his father?" "Hell nawl, I don't, Jalisa! You know that, but man, his bitch ass doesn't deserve to live after all this pain he's causing her." "She loves that dog so much that she tried to take her own life." "I know, but you can't let this drive you to evil and damage the bond you'll have with your nephew." "I told you I don't have to touch the punk. I'll just put 10 bands on his head and let one of them lil niggas from the block knock him off. That way, my hands will be clean, and Aiden won't have a reason to hate me, unless someone runs their mouth." "Choc!! You're being irrational right now. Just let it go so we can be here for our sister. You know when she gets out the hospital, she's going to need us more than ever, and we both need to be here for her. We have to help her get strong again and see that life goes on after heartbreak." We both burst out laughing at the thought of Jalisa being the logical one in this situation. "Look at the hot head ghetto queen talking with good sense. You were the fighter of the crew, always in some shit, now you trying to talk me out of killing somebody." "You're right, but I'm grown now all that shit I did back in the day was dumb. I'm glad none of it had a real major impact on my life. You know I don't know where I would be without you and Redbone. I was living wild and reckless!

To be continued….